The Flowers Need Watering

Marcus Lopés

TORONTO, CANADA

Marcus Lopés
Toronto, Ontario
Canada

First Edition

Book Layout © 2017 BookDesignTemplates.com
Cover Design: Lieu Pham
www.covertopia.com

Library and Archives Canada Cataloguing in Publication

Lopés, Marcus, author

The flowers need watering / Marcus Lopés.

Issued in print and electronic formats.

ISBN 978-0-9958294-0-4 (softcover).--ISBN 978-0-9958294-1-1 (PDF)

I. Title.

PS8623.O635F56 2017   C813'.6   C2017-900611-8

C2017-900612-6

For friendships past and present,

and those still to come.

The Flowers Need Watering

TUESDAY

1

"WHAT?" MATEO BARKED INTO THE PHONE, BUT THE ONLY response was the deafening blare of the dial tone. In the darkness, his eyes half-open, he fumbled to return the phone to the nightstand. He rolled onto his back and lay there, still, trying to catch his breath. His eyes were fully open now, acclimatized to the dark and fixed on the ceiling. He drew in long, deep breaths, one after the other. He could feel his heart rate slow, the tightness in his chest easing. He shifted onto his right side, his gaze falling on the bright red digits of the clock next to the phone. Twenty-six minutes past three. "Christ!" He violently shoved the counterpane away, huffing with each movement, and sat up on the edge of the bed.

Mateo turned on the bedside lamp and squinted. A call in the middle of the night was like a sucker punch. It always took him time to get his breath back, to shake off the anxiety. Doubly so on a night like this — when he was alone. He turned to examine the other side of the king-size bed. It was relatively untouched, except for the odd foray his feet had made. Had there been an accident? Was Simon okay? Mateo massaged the area above his heart. Panic burned in his chest the way it always did after eating a spicy bowl of chili. He was confident that, this time, Tums wouldn't provide any relief.

There was no way Mateo was going back to sleep. He moved off the bed and collected the blue and white striped pyjama bottoms that were bunched in a ball by the door. He was about to put his right leg through the leg hole when the shrill of the phone ricocheted off the walls. He staggered, pulled on the pyjama bottoms and rushed to answer the phone. "What is it?" was his harsh greeting on the third ring.

"Mateo?" the gruff voice asked.

"Yes."

"It's Ryan."

Mateo's body went rigid. He did his best to tamp down the irritation. There he was again trying to recover from the sucker punch delivered by a call in the middle of the night. That the call was from his older brother only compounded the shock. Brothers by blood, strangers by choice, Mateo and Ryan hadn't spoken to each other in nine years. What news was so bad that Ryan had to break the code of conduct?

"What's going on, Ryan?" Mateo's words were drained of all emotion.

"Dad's in the hospital," Ryan said, his voice lifeless, like a man already in mourning. "It doesn't look good. We've been advised to call the family home. Everyone —"

"All right. Thanks for the call."

"Did you hear what I said?" Ryan ignored the voice in the background urging him to calm down. "Dad is —"

"Thanks for the call." Mateo hung up and lowered himself onto the bed. He couldn't move, couldn't outrun the thorny past unleashed by the churlish voice. A past Mateo had fled. A past he had wiped from his memory. A past he didn't want to unearth.

Some people believed that family was everything. Mateo Borden was not one of those people. Ryan's call reminded him of that. Mateo was the youngest, perhaps even a mistake. The outcast. His sister called him a rebel. Adoptee, his brothers often teased, but in his adolescence Mateo could see a semblance of truth in that long-running quip. His strong, sturdy nose, his low brow, his dark brown eyes and the caramel hue of his skin offered physical proof that he was part of the Borden clan, part of *them*. As did his name: Matheus Richard Borden. Matheus and Richard were the names of his two grandfathers who had both died before he was two. Yet his name didn't hold him, in a meaningful way, to his family, didn't solidify the link. "Be who *you* want to be," his sixth-grade teacher often repeated. *Change your name*, was how Mateo had translated that. He started calling himself Mateo, despite his parents' vocal disapproval. He liked to think that that was the moment he became a man. In truth it was the manifestation of his long-simmering discontent with his parents' "rule" and the first phase in a mutiny that would shake the family to its core. The precursor to a break that had, rather effectively or so he believed, untangled himself from the suffocating web of family.

A chill shot through Mateo's spine. He moved off the bed and went to the dresser. He took a white T-shirt from the third drawer and pulled it on as he left the bedroom and made his way to the darkness downstairs. In the kitchen, he turned on the light and retrieved a glass from the upper cupboard in the corner by the stove. He thought about having a glass of orange juice but knew he needed something stronger and shot into the dining room. He returned a moment later carrying the bottle of Lagavulin and poured a generous amount of the golden liquid into his glass. He drained it and winced as his throat burned. He poured himself another, larger drink, picked up his glass and made for his office. He had just sat down at his desk when the phone rang. He took a sip of his scotch and reached for the receiver. "What, now?"

"Now that's no way to speak to your favourite sister," the sultry voice scolded.

"Sorry, Melinda," Mateo said. "The call with Ryan earlier still has me on edge."

"Why aren't you here at the hospital?" Melinda said askance. "You should be here."

Mateo didn't know how to respond and remained silent. Melinda was the only one of his siblings who he saw as his ally, his friend. She was also his biggest fan and had created the Mateo Borden Fan Page on Facebook. It had over one million likes from his faithful readers. Mateo and Melinda got along because they were both rebels, both took paths that had contradicted their mother's will. Melinda taught Grade 12 history at a local high school and had married the love of her life, Zane Grey, when she was nineteen. No one talked about the fact that Melinda was pregnant, in her third trimester, when she walked down the aisle. They couldn't deny that Melinda and Zane were absolutely ecstatic. Even so, their parents were not enthusiastic about the pregnancy or the marriage. Zane's parents had tossed about the idea of adoption, but both Zane and Melinda wanted to keep the child. And keeping the child, according to Melinda's parents, meant marriage. Melinda was hell-bent on going to university and making something of herself. Having a baby wasn't going to hold her back. If anything, it motivated her to succeed. She wasn't going to be, as her mother often alluded, another sad statistic.

"I don't know what you mean," Mateo said.

"He's your father."

"Biologically speaking, yes."

"Fuck off, Mateo."

"Melinda —"

"We're family."

"Says who?"

"I do. Regardless of our differences, of what has happened in the past, we're still family."

"Not from my perspective." Mateo leaned back in his chair and pulled the phone slightly away from his ear as Melinda groaned. "Let me know if anything changes."

"Put Simon on the phone."

"He's away."

"Don't do this, Matté —"

"Mateo." Matté was another throwback to the past he wanted no part of, a reference to a deep betrayal by the only person whom he ever thought of as a best friend.

"Don't stay away. You'll regret —"

"I'm not coming," Mateo said forcefully.

"Matheus."

"Don't call me that either."

"Mateo…" Melinda's tone went from confrontational to conciliatory. "There's a real chance that Dad's not going to survive this time. You know, Mateo, here you could be the bigger man. You could, for once, be that olive branch." There was a silence, and Melinda switched back to being argumentative. "Suit yourself, but don't say I didn't warn you."

She paused, calming herself down. "I'll call you if there's a change." She hung up.

Mateo, after setting his phone down on his desk, polished off his drink and listened. There were no discernible noises, no ticking clocks, not even the sound of the leaves of the oak tree brushing against his office window. The night was still, absolutely still, but the calm would only last so long. Mateo could feel the storm approaching. He leaned forward and turned on the desk lamp. He picked up the phone again and dialled the number he had long ago committed to memory.

"Hello," the groggy voice said.

"I'm so sorry," Mateo said. "I shouldn't have woken you —"

"It's okay. Is everything all right?"

"Peter's in the hospital." Mateo sipped his drink. "Apparently it doesn't look good, but I…" He paused, lifting his glass to his mouth again. Then he said, "Simon, I can't go there. I can't —"

"All right," Simon said in a comforting way. "I'm coming home."

"You should stay," Mateo encouraged. "You're one of the guest speakers." Simon, a professor of political science, was in Ottawa for a symposium on Canadian elections and political participation. "I just needed to hear your voice."

"They'll understand," Simon said. "Besides, I gave my presentation yesterday. I won't be missed. I'll get back as soon as I can."

"Okay." There was a silence. "Thank you."

"You know I love you, right?" Simon said.

"Yes."

"And Mateo…" There was a slight edge in Simon's voice. "You know drinking won't help."

"It's to calm my nerves, take the edge off. Don't make it sound like I'm an alcoholic."

"Just try to stay focused."

"Christ, I'm trying."

"Try to get some rest, and I'll see you soon."

Click.

The winds were gathering strength, the storm was closing in, and in the midst of it Simon would be Mateo's refuge. Like always. That made Mateo smile, instilled a certain calm. Simon had, after all and despite an awkward debut to their romance, successfully wedged his way into Mateo's life.

The day, five years ago, when Mateo and Simon had met was a Wednesday, and Mateo could still remember the way the bright June sun lit up the robin's-egg blue sky. Mateo, although at the time couldn't say why, felt like there was something "good" about the day, that it belonged to him. He was at Titles, the independent bookstore where he often shopped, leisurely roaming up and down the narrow aisles. He wasn't looking for anything in particular, but liked to stay current with other authors in his genre. Moving through the store, he regularly stepped around other patrons, and one particular tall, dark-haired beauty who seemed to always be in his way. Mateo, stopping in front of the art section, pulled out a book on Wassily Kandinsky and leafed through it. From the corner of his eye he glimpsed the black-haired man coming towards him and took a step forward to let him pass, but the man stopped and contemplated the self-help section next to the art books.

"You're Mateo Borden, right?" the deep voice said uncertainly.

Mateo, looking up from the book, nodded. He always hoped to avoid such moments, when people recognized him and began some type of inquiry. He said, "Yes," and warily accepted the man's firm handshake.

"I really enjoy your work, your last novel especially. Oh, I'm Simon Denault by the way."

Mateo returned the book on Kandinsky to the bookshelf and, turning to walk away, said, "It was a pleasure meeting you, Mr. Denault."

"Actually…" Simon moved to intercept Mateo. "I'd like to buy you a coffee." He burst out laughing at Mateo's alarmed, wide-eyed look. "You're probably thinking that I'm some kind of stalker, but I'm not. Of course I'm expecting you to take my word on that, but it's true." He let out a nervous laugh. "But I just…" Simon bit down on his lower lip as he caught the apprehension flicker in Mateo's eyes. "All right." He reached for his wallet and pulled out a white business card, which he handed to Mateo. He leaned in and whispered into Mateo's ear, "I think you have a great smile." He stepped past Mateo and headed for the exit.

Mateo fingered the card and looked in the direction of the exit, and all he saw was the back of Simon's full dark mane disappearing out of sight. He slipped the card into his jeans pocket and wondered if this was some kind of test. Most people asked for his autograph but this was different. Mateo was surprised to *feel* something, like the dark-haired beauty had stirred something inside of him. Had Mateo, whose past unsuccessful romances had him purposely avoiding the trials of love, let his guard down? Mateo rushed to the exit and stepped out onto the sidewalk, swinging his head from left to right, and then sprinted down the sidewalk towards the tall figure about to cross over Dresden Row. At the corner Mateo, gasping for breath, placed his hand in the centre of Simon's back and offered an insouciant smile when Simon looked at him. "Do you have time for that coffee now?" Mateo asked.

The phone rang again, involuntarily dragging Mateo back to the present. He didn't answer the phone. Instead he switched off the lamp, stood, and made for his bedroom, turning the kitchen light out along the way. In the bedroom, he stretched out on his bed, still wearing the T-shirt and pyjama bottoms, and groaned as his gaze fell on the clock. Two minutes to five. Most mornings he was up by six thirty. Could he fall back asleep now and for how long? He crawled under the covers and drew them snug against his body. He wasn't expecting to sleep but needed to, somehow, protect himself from the brewing tempest. He thought about his conversation with Melinda, but he didn't share her point of view. They weren't family, not in the way she meant. And even though that should have bothered him, he wasn't unsettled by it. Before long Mateo was fast asleep, his dream-world offering a temporary reprieve from a past that was about to catch up to him.

2

Liam Robertson paced the area between the white leather loveseat and the living room window, repeatedly biting down on his lower lip.

"Oh, sit down," Susan Robertson said.

Liam ignored his mother's plea to sit, and now stood with his hands shoved in his pockets. He stared blankly out the window. It was a few minutes past nine, and Susan, seated on the matching sofa, stroked her short silver hair in between sips of her green tea. She sighed, and placed her teacup and saucer on the coffee table. "Liam!"

Liam spun around and shot his mother a menacing glare that seemed to bounce off her. He pulled his hands out of his pockets and sat down on the loveseat, avoiding his mother's probing blue eyes. He knew that she was waiting for an explanation. He wasn't ready to explain, or to even admit to himself, what had brought him home so "unexpectedly." Yet they'd always been close, and didn't she deserve to know the truth? He lifted his gaze and, when their eyes met, smiled faintly.

"I think I've been patient long enough." Susan picked up the flowery teapot and refilled her cup. "Doctor Reid says I'm fine, that I'm in remission. You didn't have to come back here to take care of me." She picked up her teacup and saucer. "And I certainly don't need taking care of."

"I know that," Liam said somewhat harshly. He had been devastated by his mother's fight with breast cancer, terrified of losing the one person who loved him unconditionally his whole life. "But with Dad gone I don't like the idea of you being here on your own. This way I'll be close by if you need me." His father had died seventeen months ago, two months before his mother's cancer diagnosis. His older sister, Cassandra, became a Jehovah's Witness at twenty-six and they never heard from her again. "Besides, it felt like the right time to come home."

"I thought you loved living in New York," Susan said with a hint of surprise.

Despite her illness, Liam could still see the youthfulness in her thin, round face, and the hope that danced in her big round eyes. They shared the same straight aquiline nose and prominent cheekbones. In her youth he imagined that potential suitors saw her as a Greek goddess. She'd have thought of herself as the mortal Alcmene. *Does that make me her Heracles?*

"So did I." Liam bounced off the loveseat and began pacing the area behind it again. "I just…" He cupped his hands to the back of his head and turned to look at his mother. His hands fell to his sides and he said, "It didn't feel like home, not in the way that I wanted it to," with an air of defeat.

"Oh, Liam…" Susan returned her teacup and saucer to the coffee table and, with her left hand, patted the cushion next to her twice. "Come sit down." After Liam reluctantly sat down next to her, Susan shifted her body sideways slightly and held his hands. "You spent too many years running away from yourself, running away from who you are." She applied a little pressure. "I've only ever wanted you to be happy. I won't lie. I'm glad you're home. I worried so much about you living in that city, especially after… Well, we needn't talk about *that*. But, Liam, can't you at least be honest with me? You came home for *him*."

"No, I didn't." Liam yanked his hands out of his mother's grasp, shot up off the sofa and flung himself into the club chair that was part of the living room set. He sat in the chair, slouched down with his arms folded across his chest and his full pink lips pursed tightly.

"You've always loved him. When you had the chance to be with him, or at the very least tell him how you felt, then you lacked the courage. Now you have the courage but —"

"But now he's with someone else." Liam couldn't keep his voice even, letting his annoyance seep through. He sat up straight in the chair and fixed his gaze on the dark hardwood floor. "And I did tell him, sort of…" He glanced in his mother's direction and rolled his eyes. "Oh, don't look at me like that. None of that matters now."

"Really?"

"It was complicated," he snapped.

"Complicated."

"Don't do that."

She smirked. "Don't do what?"

"Mother!" Liam hid his face in his hands for a moment before running them through his full blond mane. "Maybe you're right. I want to see him, find out how he's doing. I never liked how we left things. But I didn't come back for that. I came for you."

"You were never much of a liar," Susan said. "And you could have found out how he's doing from New York. You didn't have to uproot your entire life."

"I thought you were glad to have me back?"

"That's not the point. As for how *you* left things —"

"I had to *do* something." Liam brought himself forward, sat on the edge of the chair and looked at his mother. "I felt lost in the city, lost in my work. Nothing mattered anymore." He suppressed the defeat rising in his voice. "All I ever wanted was to feel like I was doing something important, that I was making a difference in the world. I didn't … I don't feel that. All that I was really doing was shifting papers about." He shrugged. "And, yes, I know how *I* left things between me and…"

"You can't even say his name."

Liam sat back in the chair, his eyes moist, his mind inundated with images of the man he had wanted to love a lifetime, and still did.

"What are you going to do *now*?" Susan asked pointedly. "You're not going to sit around here and mope all day, are you? That's all you've done since you've been home."

"I'm going to check out a couple of condos with Dan this afternoon. Maybe I'll buy one where I can mope free of persecution."

They laughed.

Susan placed the teapot, along with the teacup and saucer, on the wooden tray resting on the coffee table and picked it up as she stood. She went over to Liam and, balancing the tray in her left hand, cupped her right hand to his shoulder. "I don't think that you should put off seeing him. The sooner you see him, the sooner you'll have some of the answers you're seeking. Then you'll know what to do." She squeezed his shoulder and left the room.

Alone in the living room and embalmed in a disconcerting silence, Liam was invaded by a new and profound anxiousness. "What the fuck am I going to do?" he mumbled, and ran his hand over his face. After almost a month since his mother had collected him and his baggage from the airport, Liam was still putting off decisions, putting off life. What was coming home supposed to give him? Answers. A way forward. There was only one problem. Liam was too afraid to ask the necessary questions, too terrified of getting back to the core of things.

Liam was in mourning for the home he had wanted New York to be, a sort of haven. Yet, in eight years, he was never truly swept up in its opulence and power, never fell under the city's spell. To his family and friends the move to New York was glamorous and prestigious. Not so glamorous were the twelve-hour days he put in in his advisory role in mergers and acquisitions. Broadway. Times Square. Staten Island. Battery Park. These were big-name landmarks that eluded him until his last week in the city when he was free of his job, free of a world that had succeeded at unmaking him.

He left New York ravaged by disappointments, but while he was there his Tribeca loft-style apartment on Franklin Street was his sanctuary. The ten-foot ceilings made him feel like he could breathe in a city that often felt suffocating. Located on the top floor of his building, his large private balcony helped him to feel free when he often felt confined. He came to appreciate the open chef's kitchen since he spent most of his free time trying to become a "master" of French cuisine by working his way through Julia Child's cookbooks, and reading Robert Ludlum novels. Sometimes he went for dinner at The Dutch in Soho and imagined himself becoming a regular, but he didn't like eating out alone. He worried that gave the impression that he was unworthy, or incapable, of love. Not just that. He tried dating, but the long hours he put in at the office made guys suspicious — that he couldn't commit, or that he was playing the field, or that the only thing that mattered was his work. No one seemed to trust him. Were they right? Maybe he couldn't commit. No, he didn't want to commit. His heart was forever pining over a love that had withered without a real chance to bloom. He didn't trust himself. Maybe without even knowing, Liam gave up on trying to make a life for himself there.

It was, after all, partially true that he could not handle the stress of his job. It had worn him down, left him unfulfilled and, worst of all, lonely. There was also, and he didn't like to talk about it, the September eleventh attacks on the World Trade Center that rattled him. He was still rattled by those events, from time to time awakened in the middle of the night by nightmares about it that left him breathless and sweaty. He was on his way to his Center Street office at the time the first plane hit the North Tower. That was all he ever told people, unable to reveal other details. His mother had pleaded with him in the days that followed to move home but he *had* to stay. Staying was *necessary* to show his solidarity and to prove, most importantly to himself, that he wasn't afraid. But he was. Afraid.

Susan's humming of "Country Gardens" carried from the kitchen into the living room and Liam rose to his feet. He walked down the hall to the room that had been his father's office, each step weighed down by regret. He slumped into the chair behind the large cherry wood desk and opened his laptop. He intended to search the online classifieds for work or an organization where he could volunteer his time, but instead stared absently at the screen. A week ago, he met Kent Logan for lunch. Kent, well-connected to the law community's gossip line, was one of the senior partners at the first firm where Liam had worked after finishing law school. Kent tried to remind Liam about the reasons why he became a lawyer. Helping those who couldn't defend themselves. Upholding the principles of equality and fairness. Liam couldn't remember when he stopped listening, but those arguments, along with a generous financial offer, didn't sway him. He was left totally uninspired. Yet he had no idea if he wanted to continue in law or if it was time for him to do something completely different. Could he become a chef? Could he see himself running the kitchen at the Lord Nelson Hotel? Was that the life of service he envisioned for himself?

I have to see him. But what if he doesn't want to see me? He closed his laptop. "Oh, God…" He covered his face with his hands. He felt helpless and weak, like he had felt for most of his adult life. He uncovered his face, sat back in his chair and sighed. A heavy grey weight pressed down on his chest, and he thought, briefly, that he would cry. He didn't. "Fuck."

He reached for the book on the desk next to his laptop, flipped it open to the page he had marked and lost himself in that other world, one more time putting off important decisions, putting off life.

3

AT TEN PAST NOON, MATEO WAS WAITING AT THE AIRPORT for Simon to walk through the frosted sliding glass doors that opened and closed at irregular intervals. He frowned at the people who did emerge through the doors, sporting giddy smiles and rushing towards those there to greet them, and was eager to feel Simon's strong arms around him. Witnessing how mothers and fathers welcomed home their children who had been away for months had him teetering between sanity and extremity. Was that what family looked like? Was that how his parents acted with his other siblings?

Mateo yawned and glanced at his watch. Three minutes had passed since the last time he checked. The blare of the phone at nine thirty had, one more time, shattered his sleep. Another sucker punch that made his heart race, his breathing shallow. He let it ring and worked to control his breathing. The muscles in his shoulders were knotted, and he couldn't shake the wave of exhaustion rolling over his body. He yawned again, and sat down on a vacant bench that didn't block his line of vision to the sliding glass doors.

Two minutes later, the frosted glass doors slid open and Simon appeared showing off his broad, generous smile. Mateo bounced off the bench and rushed at him, like a blitz, almost literally tackling him. They kept their balance, Mateo wrapping his arms around Simon's slender body and Simon matching the intensity of the embrace. Mateo buried his face in Simon's neck, inhaling the rich, sweet notes of leather and orange blossoms. The queasiness Mateo felt earlier was replaced by a reassuring calm. When they pushed apart, they looked intently at each other and broke out into giddy laughter when they realized they'd attracted the attention of those around them. Mateo grabbed the handle of Simon's suitcase and led the way to his black Audi A6 on the third level of the parking garage.

As Mateo went to flip the engine, Simon grabbed his arm and said, "Has there been any change?"

"No," Mateo said as the engine roared, although he hadn't checked the messages before leaving for the airport. "Melinda said she'd call if things…"

"Let's stop at the hospital and —"

"Absolutely not." Mateo shifted the car into reverse and backed out of the parking spot. "If hell is other people, that would be hell." He slipped the car into drive and zoomed towards the highway.

"It's your family, your father —"

"Simon…" *Do I have to explain it again? Was he not listening the first time?* "You're my family."

"Yes, of course." Simon reached over and placed his hand on Mateo's thigh. "But what if —"

"No what-ifs," Mateo interrupted, his foot pressing down on the accelerator. They were speeding down Highway 102, the trees passing in a blur, unrecognizable, like Mateo's life, changed so abruptly years ago.

Simon trained his gaze at Mateo. The stony silence made his throat constrict. He ran his hand back and forth over Mateo's thigh. "Mateo —"

"You've forgotten what my family's like." The car gathered more speed. "Let me remind you then."

Simon sat quietly and listened.

It was the summer before Mateo's final year of university. He was twenty. He had, by this point, left the family home and was sharing a house with four other students on Walnut Street. While his tuition was covered by a full scholarship from his university, during the summer break he worked two full-time jobs to keep his landlord happy and away. He was a diligent student, dedicated to his studies because if he let his grades fall it wasn't just his scholarship that was in jeopardy. It was his life. He couldn't imagine moving back "home" after escaping his mother's clutches. But moving out came with strings attached, and he had to promise to have dinner with his parents one night a week. That night became Thursday.

On this particular rainy Thursday evening in early July, Mateo was relieved to see that his Aunt Deidre was joining them. Deidre was his father's older sister and was recovering from her devastating divorce. As was customary, Mateo's mother, Doris, dominated the conversation. Like a zealous sportscaster calling out the play-by-plays, she recounted her week's activities. Her solo, during church choir practice, that had everyone in tears. Her pies and cookies, already in the freezer, that she'd be donating to the upcoming Youth Fellowship bake sale. Planning next week's revival services that would, she believed, restore the faith of so many lost souls. If Deidre tried to interject, offer a different interpretation of the events, Doris raised her voice as if to silence her critics. Peter, who struggled to connect with his youngest son, spoke only when asked directly for his opinion, which wasn't often.

When Doris paused to sip her ginger ale, Deidre said, "You know I'm the last one to gossip, but I saw the funniest thing the other day."

"What was that, Aunt Deidre?" Mateo asked, and popped a piece of lasagna into his mouth.

Deirdre's eyes roamed the faces around the table as she spoke. "I had my appointment with my therapist Tuesday afternoon. It was late, at four, so by the time I was done it was suppertime. Those sessions leave me heavy, so I decided to treat myself to a nice dinner out."

"There was a time," Doris said, "when we didn't reveal all our shameful secrets. We were circumspect."

"I'm not ashamed," Deidre said. "After what I've been through —"

"Where did you go for dinner?" Mateo asked.

"Oh, well…" Deidre smiled. "I discovered this cosy restaurant on Spring Garden Road called Il Mercato. Such great food and delightful service. And the wine!" She licked her lips. "Peter, you simply must go."

"Wine?" Doris threw Deidre a knowing look. "You know full well Peter doesn't drink. And you shouldn't either. That's the Devil's drink. Pure poison. I tell you, these days —"

"Aunt Deidre, you said you saw something funny." Mateo flicked his eyebrows. "What was it?"

"I had a table in the corner with a view of the entire restaurant," Deidre said. "At the table in the opposite corner, I saw this young man who looked so familiar. Handsome as ever. I couldn't keep my eyes off him."

"Aunt Deidre on the prowl." Mateo winked.

Deidre waved him off and continued. "I knew I recognized him but I just couldn't place him. You know how it is. You know you know the person but can't come up with the name. Well, it wasn't until the server brought me my lemon gelato that it dawned on me. It was Zane's friend, although I still can't remember his name."

"Which friend?" Peter asked.

"The one who's always showing up at our family gatherings," Deidre said.

"Liam," Doris said disapprovingly.

Deidre snapped her fingers. "Yes!"

"What was so funny about seeing Liam at Il Mercato?" Mateo reached for his glass of water. "People eat out all the time."

"I remember Zane telling me, not too long ago, that Liam got engaged," Deidre said. "To another law student. Some girl with a funny name. Oh, that doesn't matter. It's just that…" Deidre bit down on her lips. "Liam was with a guy."

"A guys' night out," Peter said. "What's so funny about that?"

"No, no." Deidre's voice dropped. "He was *with* the guy. They were holding hands across the table."

Mateo sat up straight. "What?"

Deidre's eyes were fixed on Mateo. "You spend a lot of time at Melinda and Zane's. Has Liam ever come onto you?"

The heat rose in Mateo's cheeks.

"Deidre!" Doris gasped, placing her hand on her bosom.

"Maybe he's trying to figure it out before he gets married," Deidre said. "Better that than having your husband leave you for another man." She nodded at Mateo. "What do you think?"

Mateo shrugged. "I … I don't know Liam that well."

Doris pointed with her fork at Mateo. "Now I want you to stay away from him. You don't need that kind of influence in your life."

"Liam's not a serial killer," Deidre said, sighing. "He's gay. Or he might be … oh, what's the word? Bisexual. That doesn't make him a bad person or suggest he couldn't be a positive influence on Mateo. Like I said, I just thought it was funny because he was supposed to be engaged." She laughed. "Times sure have changed since we were young. Right, Peter?"

"Oh, I know times have changed." Doris adjusted herself on her chair. "We're supposed to be politically correct these days. Nobody wants to offend nobody. I mean, Liam seems like a nice enough young man, but if he's into any of that funny business, I can tell you that the problem was his up-bringing. It always is."

Deidre raised an eyebrow. "Well, I don't think —"

"His father probably walked out on him and his mama before he could remember," Doris said, her voice gaining momentum as if she were the preacher on a high as she delivered the Sunday morning sermon. "When a young boy has no male influence, no role model, it goes without saying that the boy's going to struggle through life. He's going to make some bad choices."

"Actually, Liam's parents are still together," Mateo said quietly. "They've been married for something like twenty-six years." He felt sick. He just proved he did know Liam well. Had his mother caught on to that?

"Being gay isn't a choice," Deidre said, shaking her head. "There's so much pressure on our young people to be this or that. Maybe Liam's just at a point where he can finally let himself be who he really is. There's nothing shameful in that."

"There's shame all right." Doris gulped the last mouthful of her drink. "I know they say being gay isn't a choice, that there's some gene responsible for it all. But if you've been brought up in the church, anchored yourself in the Word of God…" She raised her left hand in the air, testifying, like she did during Wednesday night prayer service. "You cannot be tempted. But there is shame when you let yourself be guided by the world, when you turn your back on His word. Tell them, Peter."

Peter leaned back in his chair. "Oh, well, you know, dear, the Bible says a lot of things. And you know it better than I do. I think that what's important is for us to be kind and love each other."

"Oh, I don't know anymore." Doris sounded exhausted. "You're right, Deidre. Times have certainly changed. It feels like modern society has created this free-for-all and we're losing our way. Only no one can see it. Men loving men. Women loving women. Dear Lord, what's next?"

Deidre swung her head in Mateo's direction. "How are you and your friends dealing with all these changes? Gay marriage. Assisted suicide. And, you know, legalized marijuana isn't that far off."

"I guess, um…" Mateo shrugged. "We don't see the big deal. Like Dad said … if we can be kind and love each other, and if people are happy —"

"Do you see? We've made it so nothing's a big deal now." Doris levelled her eyes at Deidre. "Doesn't matter if it goes against the scriptures. Maybe in today's society there's no longer any divide between moral and immoral. But I *believe*. In Jesus. In the afterlife. In His word. I know the Bible says —"

"Nobody really cares what the Bible says!" When Mateo realized he had actually spoken the words instead of keeping them inside his head, he froze. He held his gaze to his empty plate and drew in a long, deep breath. Then he slowly lifted his head, his mother's wild eyes on him. "I'm sorry. That just slipped out. It wasn't what I meant. Not exactly…"

"What do you mean, Mateo?" Deidre winked.

"I mean…" *Oh, my God. She knows!*

"Certainly, Matheus, if you have an opinion…" Doris leaned forward. "By all means, share it."

Mateo looked down, unable to stop his right knee from bouncing up and down. "It's just … well, you know…"

"No, I don't know," Doris said. "So tell me."

"Never mind," Mateo said, feeling like his stomach was about to flip.

Deidre rammed her foot into Mateo's under the table. "Speak up, Mateo. Now's the time."

Mateo's eyes widened. *She really does know. Christ!* "All right … it just seems … old-fashioned to think of being gay like it's some terrible sin. Maybe not old-fashioned but rather … unjust." He caught his mother's raised-eyebrow look but continued. "I mean, technically, the homeless man I saw eat a bagel in Loblaws yesterday was stealing. He might have been starving, but it was a sin, too, right? So is that a lesser sin that two men in love? And what about Uncle Terrence's affair with Aunt Tanya?"

"Matheus!" Peter's rough voice thundered a warning.

"What? Aunt Tanya sleeping with Aunt Deidre's husband isn't a sin?" Mateo asked.

"It's not the same thing," Doris said.

"Maybe it is," Deidre conceded.

"Then it's me." Mateo fell back in his chair. "But doesn't it seem like there's this, I don't know, sliding scale for sin? It's like, well, um … like a sin can be somehow less or more of a sin than others."

Doris, setting her knife and fork down on her plate, stared quizzically at Mateo. "You *can* choose between good and evil, right and wrong —"

"We don't choose who we fall in love with. It just happens." Mateo sighed. "And who says it's wrong?"

Doris's beady hazel eyes widened and, by the bug-eyed look, it seemed that she might have suffered some type of attack. Then she started blinking magnificently as she searched for words. Mateo's "sudden" brazenness had stunned. She said, "I told your father that I didn't want you living in that house with those unsaved boys. But your father said you had to grow up, learn to be independent. Now look at you. You've become a man of the world." She shook her head. "How did Satan get such a mighty grip on you?"

Mateo rolled his eyes. "Satan has about as much a grip on me as your God."

"This is getting good," Deidre said, smirking, and sat back in her chair.

Peter flashed his sister a reproachful look and then focused on his son. "Now, Matheus, it's one thing to state your opinion, but I'll not have you speak to your mother like that."

"All I'm saying," Mateo said, "is that I don't want to let myself be blinded by religion or caught up in some dogma. And it's Mateo."

"Preach it, Mateo." Deidre slapped her hand on her leg. "Preach it."

Peter pointed his fork at Mateo. "I'm not going to warn you again."

"I don't think you ever truly believed," Doris said, indignant. "And now you seem too eager to give yourself over to ungodly things."

"Maybe you're right." Mateo gave a languid shrug. "Or maybe … maybe I'd like to believe, if I had to believe in your concept of God, that God is in fact love. I mean … I could believe in a God who loves us all no matter what. *Your* concept of God, it seems to me, can wheel and deal on who to love or not to love."

"Amen," Deidre said.

"Stay out of it, Deidre," Peter growled.

"The believer will have everlasting life," Doris said.

"You don't know that for sure." Mateo drew in several deep breaths, his racing heart slowing down. He waited until he had his breath back, then locked his eyes on his mother. "All I know is that for the past six months I've been dating a guy named Spencer Fromm and 'God' hasn't struck us down yet."

There was a silence, a bone-chilling silence that swept through the dining room. Deidre's round face lit up with satisfaction. Doris blinked rapidly and Peter stared into his plate. Mateo, watching as tears flooded his mother's eyes, felt guilt and remorse, which were immediately washed away by a sweeping sense of freedom. He never planned on telling his parents that he was gay, and certainly not like this. But in the moment he had been moved, perhaps in the same way that some people were moved by the Holy Spirit — that then, in that precise moment, he had to testify.

Doris, unable to look at her son, said into her plate, "I … I think you should leave."

"Oh, Doris," Deidre said. "That's a bit much."

Doris, who was agape at Deidre's remark, recoiled in her seat. Holding her gaze to Deidre, she reached for her husband's hand and said to Mateo, "This is our house. Our house. Our rules. Our beliefs. If you can't accept…"

Mateo, caught off guard by his mother's ruthless bluntness, realized he was standing. He felt numb as his eyes became moist. He looked at his father, who on the "moral" issues always conceded to Doris's position. Peter never looked up from his plate. Mateo, curbing the urge to cry, slinked out of the house. That was the day he closed the door on family, on what family was supposed to mean.

Swerving onto the ramp leading to the Macdonald Bridge, Mateo glanced at Simon. "Do you still think it'd be a good idea to go to the hospital?"

They laughed.

"Yes, I think you should be there," Simon said.

"It's been too long. What would I say?"

"I don't think you'd have to say anything. Being there would be enough."

"It would be insufferable. And it would inevitably lead to some sort of confrontation."

"You don't know that." Simon covered his mouth as he yawned. "I can't imagine that, during a time like this, anyone would want a confrontation. You need to be there."

"Absolutely not," Mateo said over the squealing of the back tires as the car took off through the bridge's toll booth.

4

THE ELEVATOR DOORS SLID OPEN AND MATEO, FEELING SI-
mon's hands on his back, was ready for the shove. He stum-
bled into the corridor and stiffened. His nose burned with
the scent of disinfectant, which wasn't strong enough to cut
through the stomach-turning whiff of urine and feces. He
coughed and, grimacing, turned to Simon, who shrugged. Mateo had planned to press the "G" button as soon as the elevator
doors opened and flee before anyone had seen him. Simon
had thwarted his plan. Whose side was he on, anyway?

"I know that look," Simon said in a low voice. "But we're
here. Let's find Melinda and get an update. Stop trying to
imagine the worst."

"It doesn't take much imagining," Mateo said under his
breath, and his eyes shot daggers when Simon pinched his
side.

"Oh, Mateo, you've come," the familiar voice called out.

Charging towards Mateo and Simon was a tall, slim woman with short curly black hair. As she neared, she stretched
out her bare, toned arms and threw herself at Mateo.

"I'm so glad you're here," Melinda said into Mateo's ear.
They pushed apart and she hugged Simon. "Thanks for getting him here."

"How's your father?" Simon asked.

"The doctor says he's stable," Melinda said, and looked as if she were about to cry. She was about half an inch shorter than Mateo, and had the same caramel-coloured skin. She rubbed her wide-apart round eyes to prevent the tears from flowing. Like Mateo, she had their father's sturdy nose, and her full lips were painted a rich ruby red. "We haven't heard anything for about an hour now."

"There's your update," Mateo said to Simon. "Let's go." He dodged past Simon and pressed the elevator button.

Simon grabbed him by the arm and led him a short distance down the corridor, out of Melinda's earshot. He cupped his hands to Mateo's shoulders and stared intently at him. "We're not leaving yet."

"I can't do this." Mateo's eyes were moist. "It doesn't feel right. I don't belong here."

"He's your father."

"I don't think of him like that."

"Mateo!"

"What?" At the touch of a warm hand on his arm, Mateo flinched. "Oh, Jesus, Melinda."

Melinda raised an eyebrow. "Language." She searched for Mateo's hand. "You're wrong. You do belong here because we're family. Don't interrupt. I'm talking about you and me. Forget about the rest of them. I want you here. I need you here."

Simon removed his hands from Mateo's shoulders and reached past Melinda to shake the hand of the tall man who had come up quietly behind them. "Good to see you, Zane."

"Likewise, Simon," Zane said at the release of the handshake. At six-foot-four, Zane towered over everyone. He was good-looking but had filled out somewhat since university. He kept his brown hair cut short to conceal the bald spot on the top of his head. His salt and pepper goatee made him look rough, like he had just been released from prison, but everyone knew he was a pussycat. Even Doris liked him, despite him being white and having knocked up her only daughter out of wedlock. He wrapped his arm around Melinda's waist. "This heart attack might just be it. I know Peter's a fighter, but…"

Simon nudged Mateo in the side. "Maybe you should try to see him."

"Mama's with Dad now," Melinda said. "He's only allowed a couple of visitors at a time. The rest of us are waiting in the lounge."

"Then now's the perfect time to grab a coffee." Mateo took a step towards the elevators but Melinda intercepted him.

"Mateo…" She reached for his hand and led him towards the lounge, Simon and Zane following behind.

Mateo, his eyes roving the white-walled room, stood close to Melinda. He swallowed hard as a silence fell over the room. No one was talking. All eyes were on him. He looked down. He was the target and they were taking aim. It was like a scene out of *Matlock* — Mateo on the witness stand giving his version of the events, but he knew instantly that the jury had already decided on a verdict. The sentence would be just: an eternity in Tartarus. In that moment, the idea of that deep abyss offered more comfort than being in the presence of his "family." He felt ill, in a spiritual way, and wanted to back out of the room but Simon was standing directly behind him, intentionally it seemed, cutting off his escape route.

"Uncle Mateo!" the excited, cracking voice said, and from the back of the room came a fair-skinned, blue-eyed, curly-haired brunette. He flung himself at Mateo's waist.

"Hey there, Xavier," Mateo said, loosely hugging his nephew.

Xavier was quick to find Simon and hug him too, which seemed to only add to the awkwardness in the room.

Mateo glimpsed the woman with black and grey curly hair across the room. Their eyes met and he smiled. Even though the lines in her dark complexion told the story of a tattered life, he saw the joy radiating in her eyes. That always made him smile on the inside. He watched as she came towards him, moving awkwardly at first, like her joints locked up with each movement. Arthritis? There was more life in her steps as she neared Mateo and grinned. It was that mischievous smile that Mateo had depended on after the falling out with his parents. Mateo accepted her clutching embrace.

"Look at you," Deidre said proudly when the hug was over. "Handsome as ever." She contemplated Mateo who, secretly, had always been her favourite nephew. Then she shoved him playfully. "Where have you been? You and Simon were supposed to come over for supper. That was a month ago." She waved off his stuttered apology. "Excuses, excuses." She held his hands. "So glad you came. Despite everything. So glad you came." Deidre limped her way back across the room and sat down.

Mateo and Simon stepped off to the side and leaned up against the wall. Mateo's eyes roved the room, and in the worn and sullen faces he recognized his brothers, long absent from his life. In the far-right corner of the room was Ryan, the eldest of the children. He stood five-eleven, was thin, some would say sickly, and had their father's dark chocolate complexion. He kept his tight curls cut short but didn't try to hide the fact that he was balding. Even before Mateo had come out, the nine-year age difference had created a wedge. They belonged to different generations, and their ways of seeing the world were too divergent to facilitate any type of coming-together. It didn't help, either, that Ryan had become a hard-nosed, unflinching, evangelical preacher.

Standing next to Ryan was Benjamin, who was four years younger than Ryan. Benjamin was tall, his skin a pumpernickel hue, and had short hair. He had, unlike Mateo and Ryan, a muscular build. Where age and religion separated Mateo and Ryan, distance was what kept Benjamin and Mateo apart. Benjamin had fled to Toronto at eighteen to study, rarely returning home to visit. He was a psychiatrist at Mount Sinai Hospital. Three years ago he married a woman named Betty Wilson. Actually, they eloped with only Melinda and Zane as witnesses. Mateo learned from Melinda that when Benjamin finally brought Betty home to meet the family, their mother constantly referred to Betty as "lovely." That made Mateo chuckle. Lovely was code for, "She's white," and "How dare a son of mine marry some skinny, shapeless white girl." Benjamin stood holding the hand of a slim, pale-white woman. *That must be her.*

Mateo tried to stay calm, to curtail the anxiousness trying to invade his body, but that was hard to do as people were sneaking, and not so discreetly, sidelong glances of him and Simon.

He heard a movement behind him and his eyes shifted towards the door. Doris appeared beside a tall woman with freckles and short straight red hair. Doris glimpsed Mateo to her left when she came fully into the room. She looked critically, and with disbelief, at him. Her beady eyes still carried her disappointment and hurt, and asked the question no one dared to ask: Have you cast off that demon? Mateo wasn't fazed. He met her with a hard, dismissive gaze that made her glance away.

The tall redhead looked at Mateo and said, "Oh, Mr. Borden," with a mix of surprise and excitement. "I didn't realize it was *that* Borden family. Now it all makes sense." She extended her thin hand to Mateo. "I'm Dr. Reese, and I'm attending to your father. Peter is your father, right?"

Mateo pushed his pursed lips from side to side, then winced when Simon elbowed him in the side. "Oh, well, sure. He's my father."

"Yes, well…" Dr. Reese looked about the room and said, "The bottom line is that the medication isn't working like we had hoped." She fixed her gaze on Mateo. "We need to see where the blockages are, so Peter's on his way for a coronary angiogram. I'm not optimistic at this point that we can avoid surgery. Of course we'll know more after the angiogram, but if things are as bad as I suspect, Peter is going to need a coronary angioplasty. Basically, that means we will try to open up the blood vessels that have narrowed or are blocked, and make sure blood is flowing to the heart. But let's take it one step at a time." She touched her hand briefly to Doris's arm and left the room.

Nervous chatter erupted and it sounded like bees swarming. A deep, authoritative voice rose over the ruckus. "Excuse me, everyone. Excuse me." Ryan, who had stepped into the middle of the room, was turning around in a circle and waving his hands, trying to get everyone's attention. "Let us take a moment to offer a prayer, that the Lord will place His healing hands upon my father and guide the doctors and nurses in their work. Please stand with me and hold hands."

"Coffee, now," Mateo said, gritting his teeth, and shoved Simon out of the room.

5

Liam got out of the black Lexus, closed the door and waved as the car disappeared down the street. He ambled up the driveway, tracing his right index finger along the side of his mother's beige Corolla, and slowed his pace. He sat down on the front steps, hunched forward, and stared absently at the chipped paint on the step under his feet. He picked at the paint, pulling up small pieces and chucking them through the railing and into the elderberry bushes.

The late afternoon sun was warm against his olive skin, and he stopped picking at the paint long enough to roll up his shirt sleeves. He was in full out crisis mode. Coming home was supposed to restore some type of order, but instead everything was falling down around him. He felt like he was in a game of Jenga as he constantly removed the wrong block that sent the structure tumbling. He couldn't seem to get anything right. Maybe that was an extreme view, but he felt like a failure, that he would never succeed at making something of himself and his life.

His mother's question kept reverberating through his thoughts. *What are you going to do now?* How long could he do nothing? How long could he stay with his mother before her nagging got to him? Anyway, it wasn't nagging. His mother, always holding him to account, was a sort of moral compass that brought him back to his centre when he strayed. While it sometimes irritated him, made him want to pull his hair out, he needed that kind of metaphysical whipping. On his own he wasn't sure he'd be able to find himself again, give his life purpose. He needed her. He needed her to stay in remission, to beat the cancer. He couldn't imagine getting through the next few weeks and months without her.

The front door swung open. Liam turned his head slightly, and from the corner of his eye he glimpsed his mother standing in the doorway. "How are you feeling?"

"I'm fine," Susan said.

"Are you sure?" He shifted his body so that his back rested against the railing and started to pick at the paint again. "Can I do anything?"

"I'm fine. And stop that." She sat down in one of the Muskoka chairs that, like the steps, needed to be repainted. "Tell me about your day. Any prospects?"

"Maybe. I don't know." Liam shrugged. "There's a condo on Lower Water Street I'm kind of interested in. I told Dan I'd call him later if I want to put in an offer."

"If you're interested." She held a beige dish towel in her right hand, then laid it across her lap. "You can stay here."

"I need my own place," he said. "Besides, you said you didn't need taking care of."

"I don't need taking care of." She paused, held her breath. "So I'll ask the question again. What are you going to do now?"

Liam cringed. He recognized his mother's flat tone that preceded a tough cross-examination. He understood where his lawyer temperament came from. Had she gone into law, they could have opened their own firm. They would have been a powerhouse.

Susan slung the dish towel over the arm of the Muskoka chair. "How many condos has Dan shown you?"

Liam hunched his shoulders. "Seven, maybe eight."

"Twelve." She winked. "Yes, I'm keeping track. What's wrong with the one on Lower Water Street?"

"I never said something was wrong with it." He rubbed his forehead. "It's fine."

"Just fine?"

"Yes," Liam said askance.

Susan stomped her right foot when Liam went to pick off more paint from the steps. "Then what *is* the issue?" A silence. "You don't know or are you afraid of the answer?" She clapped her hands to get Liam's attention. "Is this where you want to be?"

"Yes." Liam tried to control the anger that was beginning to boil. "Where else could I go?"

"You could have gone anywhere. But you came back here." She stomped her foot again. "And don't tell me it was just for me."

"Mom, I did come back for you. I'm concerned." Tears pooled in his eyes. "All right. Maybe I … I … I have to see him. I … I love him."

"Then *do* something!" Susan shouted. She waved to her neighbour who appeared in the driveway and looked concerned. "It's all good. Just honing our debating skills." The neighbour disappeared. Susan stood and snatched the dish towel off the arm of the chair. "If you're determined to stay here, stop dilly-dallying and get your own place. If that is, as you say, what you need. That way you'll be putting down roots, re-establishing yourself in the city. Part of that involves letting people know that you're back. Have you talked to Zane and Melinda at least?"

Liam scratched the side of his nose. "No. I don't want anyone to know I'm back until I'm settled. I mean, look at my life. It's a mess. I don't have any type of plan." He could live without a plan. What worried him was that his friends, Zane especially, might see him as a failure, that he wasn't able to handle the stress of his New York job. Would they probably think he had been let go?

"That's not a very compelling argument," Susan said. "If people knew that you were here, well, maybe they could help."

The telephone rang, and Susan rushed into the house to answer it. She was gone a short time and returned to say, "It's for you."

"For me?" Liam rubbed his face with his hands. "Who is it?"

"It's Zane."

It had been three months since Liam had last spoken to Zane. "Zane? Christ! Tell him I'm not here."

"You tell him." Susan disappeared into the house.

Liam was slow to stand. His heart raced as he went into the house and picked up the phone. "Hello."

"My God it is you," Zane said with surprise. "What are you doing back here? A visit?"

"Sort of," Liam said.

"I tried calling your New York number but it's no longer in service."

"What's up?"

"I'm at the hospital. It's Melinda's father. He's in a bad way. Not sure he's going to pull through this time."

"What can I do?"

"Get your ass over here," Zane said. "Melinda could use an ally. Christ, so could I."

"I, um, well…" Liam ran his hand through his hair. "Is he there?"

"Yes."

"Alone?"

"No, but isn't it time the two of you buried the hatchet? What happened between you was a lifetime ago. He's moved on, and so have you."

"I don't want to cause a scene," Liam said. *And you're wrong. I haven't moved on.*

"You won't. I'll be the referee if it comes to that."

"All right." Liam sighed. "I'll stop by in a bit."

"We're at the QEII, Infirmary site … The cardiac unit on the sixth floor. Use the Bell Road entrance."

Liam hung up and thought his legs were going to give out on him. His mother told him to do something, but was this what she meant? Was this the right moment for him to unravel the past and import it into the present? Maybe not, but he had to stop waiting for that perfect moment when the stars were aligned. He had to, according to his mother, stop dilly-dallying. Her car keys were on the writing desk. He picked them up and hollered towards the kitchen, "I'll be back in a bit."

Ten minutes later, he was at the hospital, waiting for the elevator doors to slide open and reveal what would happen next.

6

MELINDA JUMPED OUT OF HER SEAT. "OH ... MY ... GOD..." She contemplated the tall figure who entered the lounge where the Borden family was gathered. Tears rolled down her cheeks as she walked towards the smiling beauty.

"Hey, sis," Liam said, falling into Melinda's clenching embrace, and they held each other for a long time.

Melinda had a deep connection with Liam, a bond that was at times difficult to describe. But it was real, from the moment Zane had introduced them. There was something in those blue-grey eyes that held her in a trance, like she was possessed — something mysterious, something that had to be decoded but, initially, she didn't have the key. Melinda didn't necessarily believe in fate, but it seemed like her friendship with Liam was just there, established without effort, a *fait accompli*.

"How are you holding up?" Liam asked.

"Fine, fine." Melinda pulled out of the embrace. "How's your mom doing?"

"Solid like always." Liam's voice cracked. "A true rock. Not like me."

She offered an encouraging smile as she studied Liam to see how he had changed. She was drawn in again to those penetrating eyes and could see he was scheming. *What's he play-*

ing at? Now Liam was dodging her eyes, and she knew that he knew that she was onto him. All those years ago Melinda was the first to see through his mask. "I know you're gay," she had told him. "You know you're gay. The dog at the end of the hall knows you're gay. Just be yourself." That was how she earned the nickname, Sis. Melinda had been more of a sister to Liam than his own. She took a step backwards and, offering a slick smile, punched Liam in the arm. "Where in the dickens have you been? We've been calling your number in New York but it's not in service."

Liam rubbed the spot on his arm where Melinda hit him. "I know," he said ruefully. "It's a long story."

"Well, well, well," Zane said when he came into the room, and he and Liam moved to embrace each other. After the hug, Zane put Liam in a headlock, a move from their days on the university wrestling team. He released Liam and winked. "Liam Robertson in the flesh."

"I told you I'd stop by," Liam said with an edge.

Melinda reached out and pinched Zane in the side. "You *knew* this fool was in town?"

"I just found out," Zane said, and slipped his hand off Liam's shoulder. "I called his mother to see if she knew where he was and, lo and behold, the fool got on the phone."

Liam shook his head. "I'm not a fool."

"That's a debate for another time." Melinda reached for Liam's hand and squeezed it. "But it's good to see you. I was worried."

"Simon," Zane said, flagging him over. "I want you to meet a good friend of ours. This is Liam Robertson." Liam and Simon shook hands, and Zane then said to Liam, "Simon is Mateo's partner."

"Oh." Liam forced a smile. Was he standing face-to-face with his potential nemesis or an ally? "Where is the famous novelist?"

"He's in with Mr. Borden," Simon said.

Everyone in the room, who had been eavesdropping on the conversation, looked curiously at Simon. The news was unbelievable. Mateo and Peter together? There had to be some mistake.

Doris, seated next to Ryan, said, "What did he say?"

Ryan bounced out of his chair. "I'll see what's going on."

"Your father asked to see Mateo," Simon said as Ryan went to leave the room.

Ryan, ignoring the comment, disappeared into the corridor. The room remained silent.

Liam said, "I think I'll grab a coffee."

"Good idea," Zane said.

"I'll join you," Simon said.

"Wait for me." Melinda rushed to pick up her purse. She bent over and kissed the top of Xavier's head as he slept curled up in a chair, and charged after the men who were already halfway down the corridor.

7

MATEO SAT IN THE BROWN VINYL CHAIR THAT WAS PUSHED back from the bed in which Peter Borden lay. Mateo's eyes roved the small, dimly lit room as he repeatedly shifted in the chair, unable to find a comfortable position that made him feel relaxed. He clenched his teeth and drummed his fingers into the arms of the chair in time to the beep of the heart rate monitor near the head of the bed. He dropped his head slightly, his gaze fixed on his lap, and waited until his vision began to blur before blinking.

Dr. Reese had cornered Mateo as he paced the long rectangular corridor of the Cardiac Unit. He resented her "meddling," and was unmoved by her frank assessment of Peter's condition, "He'll be lucky to make it off the table." She touched Mateo's arm and said, "Matheus, Matheus, Matheus, was what he mumbled for the first hour he was in our care." Mateo looked skeptically at her and wondered if she had made that up? She had no reason to, no part in his family's histrionics. When Peter returned from his angiogram, Mateo had followed willingly as Dr. Reese escorted him to Peter's room.

He hasn't changed, was Mateo's first thought when he walked into the room and saw Peter propped up in the bed like a giant ragdoll. His short, tight curly black hair had little grey. His face seemed fuller, but the way he was positioned in the bed made it hard to tell if he had put on weight. The tubes in his nose, the intravenous in his arm, and the electrodes on his chest for monitoring his heart rhythm were all evidence of illness but Peter didn't look sick, not in the way that Mateo had imagined it. Peter, ignoring Dr. Reese's advice to rest, started talking the moment Mateo came into view. Mateo's concentration was easily broken by the muffled sounds and voices in the corridor.

"I wish it hadn't come to this." Peter winced. He sat still for a moment, coughed and sighed. "Could you please refill my cup of water?"

Mateo moved out of his chair, filled the glass with water and slid it towards the edge of the overbed table, making it easier for Peter to grab it. "Maybe you should rest."

Peter, his large dark hand shaking, lifted the glass to his dry lips and sipped the water. He returned the cup to the overbed table, almost spilling it. "Please, stay," Peter pleaded, like it was the wish of a man who knew he was dying. He kept his large brown eyes trained on Mateo who, after a moment, sat back down in the chair. "You know, you were never like your brothers and sister. Even as a baby you were just different. You never liked to be held or coddled, and as soon as you were strong enough you held your own bottle and threw a tantrum if your mother or I tried to hold it for you. Your independence drove your mother crazy but now I see how it's become your strength."

The door to the room swung open and a male nurse appeared. He smiled at Mateo and, approaching the bed, said, "I'm just going to check your blood pressure, Mr. Borden."

Mateo watched as the nurse took the sphygmometer from the wall behind the bed and wrapped the inflatable cuff around Peter's upper arm. In a moment the procedure was over, the nurse returning the instrument to the wall and then scribbling notes in Peter's chart. Mateo looked down as the nurse passed by him and exited the room.

Peter took another sip of water. His hand still visibly shook, and once again he almost spilled the water as he returned the cup to the table. "You stayed away so long. I'm not blaming you. We pushed you away. We didn't understand. At least you had Melinda and Zane and Xavier." He ran his hand over his mouth. "I want you to know that there were times when I wanted to reach out to you but I… You were so independent, so determined to do everything on your own, on your own terms. I never felt like you looked up to me. Maybe you saw me, see me now, as a weak man. Maybe you believe that I let your mother bully me." He sighed. "Maybe that's somewhat true." He looked intently at Mateo. "But I'm here, on this precipice, and I had asked the Lord to let me hang on long enough to see *you* because … I want you to know, and believe, that I'm sorry. I'm sorry, Matheus, that I wasn't there for you, that I wasn't the father you deserved."

"Peter —"

"I wish you wouldn't call me that."

"Peter," Mateo said firmly, as a way of affirming Peter's status in his life, "we can't change the past, and it doesn't do any of us any good to ruminate on it. We all made choices, and now we have to live with them. But you can't look to me for forgiveness. That's between you and your God."

"Matheus —"

"Mateo."

"This isn't about you and me. It's larger than that, larger than us. It's about *them*, your family." Peter sounded frustrated, that his words did not have the power to move, to make Mateo fully understand his position. He coughed and took a sip of water. "You might think that we tossed you to the wolves —"

"Isn't that exactly what you did?"

"Don't be like that, Matheus, er, Mateo. Don't hold on so tightly to hate." There was a silence. "When I'm gone this family will need an anchor, and that's not Ryan. He's too much like your mother." Peter lifted his trembling hand and pointed his index finger at Mateo. "You will. You'll stand up to your mother, make her see in a new way. Don't get me wrong. I've loved your mother for forty-two years. I know she's a bit zealous when it comes to religion, and that for her every issue is black and white. What you never saw, what none of you ever saw, was your mother and I battling out issue after issue. It's what made our love strong. Now I need you to take on that role."

Mateo stood. "I'm not interested."

"Mateo…" Tears rolled down Peter's face. "Your family needs you. Don't follow my lead. Don't turn your back on family."

"You should rest," Mateo said and turned towards the door.

"You're quite talented," Peter called out just as Mateo gripped the doorknob. "I'm not sure where you get it though. No one on either side of the family was ever literary-minded. Yes, I've read your books."

Mateo let go of the doorknob and spun around, disbelief in his eyes, his round mouth drooping open. "You've … read … my … books?"

"Melinda raved about them," Peter said. "Reading them was a way for me to stay connected to you, even in some minute way. I'd like to think that it also gave me a better understanding of you, how you think and see the world, if you will." A faint smile spread across his face. "I once had your idealism."

"What happened?"

"What happens to most of us," Peter said with an air of disappointment, "life. I got married, started a family and my priorities changed. I had to provide for my family. I couldn't afford to chase after silly dreams."

"Dreams aren't silly," Mateo spat.

"No, I suppose they're not." Peter shrugged. "I guess I never had the courage to chase after mine, to become the man I had imagined myself becoming. Not like you."

"That sounds like regret."

"In part, yes. But I don't regret my life with your mother, or having you kids. Those have been my greatest joys."

"All right. I'm going to let you rest."

"This is it, Mateo." Peter's voice vibrated his angst. "I know this is the end for me. I can feel it. I think it's time, anyway."

"That sounds pathetic," Mateo said, "like you're giving up, like you don't *believe*."

"I *believe*," Peter said with emphasis, "that I'm going home." Peter held out his trembling hand and, after what seemed like an eternity, Mateo stepped towards the bed and gripped it. "I'm proud of you, proud of the man you've become. I hope Simon makes you happy. Melinda raves about him, too. I hope that there's forgiveness in your heart, that you can, one day, forgive me. Please, Mateo, don't give up on *her*. Try to be the bridge —"

"Rest, Peter." Mateo pulled his hand out of Peter's weak grasp and made for the door.

Just then Ryan burst into the room, his angry eyes levelled at Mateo, who looked down and took a step towards the door.

"Mateo…" Large tears gathered in Peter's eyes as Mateo grasped the doorknob. "I love you, son."

Mateo hesitated at the words but refused to turn around. What was he supposed to say? A tear rolled down his cheek. He yanked open the door and barrelled into the corridor.

8

"Am I back for good?" Liam, walking with Simon ahead of Zane and Melinda, shrugged. They stopped in front of the nurses' station and Liam turned to face his old friends. "I don't know. I'm still trying to sort things out."

"But you're looking at condos?" Melinda asked, her tone somewhat sharp. She was still digesting the shock of Liam's reappearance and trying to figure out his game plan. "That makes it sound like it's permanent."

Liam gave a wry laugh. "You know my mother. She's been great, and I love her dearly, but staying with her is, at times, trying. I'm keeping my options open."

Melinda, Zane and Liam laughed.

Zane moved behind Melinda and held her against him. "What about work? Do you have anything lined up? Have you thought about returning to the firm?"

Liam shook his head. "I've already turned down Kent's offer."

Zane scrunched his eyebrows. "How the hell did Kent find out you were back?"

Melinda reached behind and tapped her hand playfully against Zane's butt. "Watch your language."

"Kent knows everybody," Liam said, smirking. "He must have…" His voice broke off and he staggered, quick to place his hand to the counter of the nurses' station to prevent himself from collapsing. His heart raced and his eyes widened as they locked onto the source of his hopes and dreams. There was Mateo, who had just rounded the corner but who walked with his head bowed. Was he dreaming? Was that really Mateo? Simon had moved to intercept, and Liam watched as the couple talked in hushed voices. Everything around Liam faded into the background, into blackness. Nothing existed except for the man who had yet to really see him. This was the moment Liam was waiting for, that should have filled him with joy and happiness, but he was terrified. He edged past Zane and Melinda and stopped. He breathed deeply, as if he was summoning up the courage to face down his biggest fear. He squeaked an uneven, "Mateo!" that made the hair on his arms stand up.

Mateo's head swung in Liam's direction. They shared an intent stare. Mateo touched his hand to Simon's chest, as if it were a gesture of reassurance of their bond. Then he went over to Liam, keeping about two feet between them.

Liam tried to smile but his face muscles locked. He stepped forward with his arms outstretched and drew Mateo into him. Mateo didn't immediately return the embrace, but Liam held on, feeling something shift inside of him. He nestled his nose in Mateo's neck, inhaled, and recognized the scent that drove him mad. He ran his hands down Mateo's shoulders, over his shoulder blades and stopped at his waist. That was when he felt the pressure of Mateo's arms around him, their bodies jostling into position, knowing instinctively how to move and how they fitted together. Liam was relieved to be able to hold Mateo, to feel him, be close to him, and tears filled his eyes.

Simon came up behind Mateo and cleared his throat.

Liam pulled away, taking a moment to dry his eyes.

"Liam Robertson," Mateo said, letting a small part of his suspicion seep through. "This is a —"

"Surprise," Melinda interrupted, easing out of Zane's embrace and putting herself between Mateo and Liam.

"That wasn't the word I was going to use," Mateo said, and raised an eyebrow at Liam. "What are you doing here?"

"Oh, Christ, let's not go through that again," Zane said, shoving his hands in his pockets.

Melinda pointed her index finger at Zane. "Language." She looked at Mateo. "Zane's right. That's too long of a story. He can tell you that another time. How's Dad?"

"All right," Mateo said, his gaze never leaving Liam's. "I need some air."

"I'll join you," Simon said, and followed Mateo towards the elevator.

Liam trained his gaze on Simon and Mateo huddled together in front of the elevators. With the commotion around him — a couple of the nurses laughing, Melinda asking him questions, the groan of pain coming from somewhere down the corridor — he strained to make out what Mateo was saying to Simon. A bell sounded, the elevator doors slid open, and Mateo charged in while Simon remained in the corridor. Liam looked down when Simon turned towards him, but not before seeing the disappointment knotted in Simon's face. Another bell dinged, and when Liam looked up he saw Simon rush into the elevator.

Melinda and Zane had returned to the lounge, leaving Liam standing alone in front of the nurses' station. Remembering

Mateo's questioning look and the way his eyes hurled disbe-lief, even contempt, Liam felt numb and anxious. It was like they didn't know each other at all, that their history had been wiped out. But the way they hugged, held on to each other, perfectly fitting together, was proof of their connection. *It's just the shock. It'll pass, and it'll be like old times.* Did Liam really believe that? He knew he had to, again, earn Mateo's trust.

That wasn't going to be easy.

9

Mateo was pacing the sidewalk in front of the emergency entrance, Simon was seated at a table in the cafeteria, while Melinda, Zane and Liam were in the lounge listening to Dr. Reese's update.

"We're going ahead with the surgery, to see if we can get more blood moving to the heart." Dr. Reese went over to Doris, helped her out of her chair and led her out of the lounge. "Peter has asked to see you. Say what you have to say. You'll have about ten minutes before he'll be taken away for surgery."

Melinda leaned closer to Zane. "That doesn't sound good."

"Peter's a fighter," Zane said.

"Nevertheless, we should find Mateo and let him know," Melinda said.

"I'll go," Liam volunteered, and jetted out of the room. All the way down to the main floor, Liam could feel himself trembling. Was he finally going to have some time alone with Mateo? What would he say? How would they act? With Zane, Melinda and Simon watching, he felt like his and Mateo's first interaction had been tempered, censored even, like they had to hold themselves back from doing and saying necessary things. He wanted to hold Mateo again, as if that would give him proof of the situation, that it was real and not another one of his fantasies. He exited at the nearest door and, with the early evening sun warm against his skin, strolled the perimeter of the hospital. It wasn't long before Mateo came into view, and Liam's heart began to pound so fiercely he thought it was going to pop right out of his chest.

"How are you holding up?" Liam asked.

Mateo had just sat down on the wooden bench when the question bounced in the air. Leaning forward with his forearms resting on his thighs and his hands clasped together, he took his time lifting his head in the direction of that deep, mesmerizing voice. "I'm fine," he said, his words barely audible, and stood.

Liam sat down on the bench, his eyes glued to Mateo pacing the sidewalk in front of him. "Your father's going in for surgery."

"Maybe this whole thing will be over soon," Mateo said with a hint of relief.

"What?"

"Nothing." Mateo stopped pacing and looked coolly at Liam. It had been so long since Mateo had stared into those dreamy blue-grey eyes, so long since he had thought about Liam and the friendship they had shared. "What are you doing here?"

"Zane called and told me about your father." Liam was on the defensive. "I wanted to be here for Melinda and Zane." *And for you.* "They're like family to me."

"That's not what I mean." Mateo folded his arms. "What are you doing *here*, in Halifax?"

"I don't think that now's the time —"

"Still the constant evader."

"That's not fair."

"It just seems, well … I hardly think that it's fortuitous that you're here now."

Liam, shaking his head, sat back in the bench. "Look, I came down to tell you about your father and to see how you're doing, not to be interrogated."

"Why do you care how I'm doing?" Mateo's voice cracked as he worked to push down the anger rising inside of him. The feeling wasn't new. He'd felt it seven years ago. It was Thanksgiving Monday, and he was at Melinda's playing with Xavier in the living room. "Liam looked tired," he heard Melinda say from the kitchen. "I'm worried about him." Mateo froze. *Liam! He's in town?* Tears crept into his eyes. He'd come to depend on Liam in an unexpected way. Liam took him grocery shopping, critiqued the early versions of his writing and listened to him vent about the boys he dated. Despite his earlier resistance, they became close. Like brothers. That was why he believed their friendship could survive any type of crisis. Liam had been in New York almost eight months and Mateo hadn't heard from him — no response to his e-mails or letters, none of his phone calls answered or returned. *Liam's here, in Halifax, and has reached out to Melinda, Zane and God knows who else. Just not me.* Mateo's eyes were dry. The sadness he felt transformed into disappointment, then a bitterness that had him swallowing the acidic saliva pooling in his mouth. Maybe none of it meant anything — their friendship, their bond. *I guess I didn't mean as much to him as he said,* he thought, his fingers balling into fists.

Mateo silently counted backwards from ten, and that made him feel calmer. The feeling didn't last long once his eyes were again glued to Liam. He was trapped in a constant volley between the present and the past.

"Mateo, I —"

"You left for New York and I never heard from you." Mateo unfolded his arms and shoved his hands in his pockets. "Not a phone call or e-mail, not a card on my birthday or at Christmas. When you came back to visit you purposely avoided *me* while seeing everyone else. Christ, it's like you thought I had the plague."

Liam bounced off the bench. "Matté, that's not true. Don't think that I forgot about you. I never forgot about *you*. Never."

There was a silence, and they looked searchingly at each other. Matté was a nickname Liam had created one night, early in their friendship, when they were drinking scotch and playing cards. The use of it now, after so many years, sent Mateo's mind spinning. Studying Liam, Mateo could not shake the feeling that his presence was more of a disturbance, a sort of prophetic disruption, and insidious. Liam, who was thirty-six, was good-looking with his blond cropped hair and strong straight nose. He had full pink lips that formed a firm mouth and a dimple in his chin. His almost square face gave him a rugged look that was attractive to both men and women. He was the same height as Mateo but had a more athletic build.

"Let me explain," Liam said.

"It shouldn't surprise you," Mateo said, giving free will to the rage simmering in his voice, "that I'm not interested in explanations. Yours especially."

Out of nowhere it seemed Simon appeared, unsettled by the scene and unsure of his place. He cleared his throat, and when Mateo and Liam looked at him, opened his mouth to speak but nothing came out. He tried again, and managed to get out, "Mateo … your father…"

"What about him?" Mateo said, almost shouting.

Simon walked over to Mateo and reached for his hand. "I'm so sorry…"

Mateo, staring blankly at Simon as if waiting for the punch line, said, "Oh … fuck … Christ!"

WEDNESDAY

1

Simon entered the kitchen and made a beeline for the coffeemaker. As he poured himself a cup, he noticed Mateo hunched over the table in the breakfast nook and held his breath. Did Mateo not hear his brusque movements? Or was Mateo pretending like he wasn't there? "Fuck!" Simon yelled as the hot liquid rolled over the rim of his mug and onto his hand. He set the mug down on the counter with a hard clank and cleaned up the mess. During the commotion Mateo didn't move, didn't stir, and that scared Simon. Terrified him, actually.

The tension of the night before had yet to dissipate. It had built a wall of stony silence. Leaving the hospital, Mateo didn't say a word, didn't look at Simon and, once home, he retreated to his office. Simon didn't know what to do or how to comfort him. All of Simon's attempts at consolation and comfort — a hug, a hand on the shoulder, a kiss — were spurned by Mateo, whose eyes were angry and wild and dead. Simon felt like he had been, without any warning, placed in the enemy camp. He was desperate to change that, to be Mateo's ally again.

Simon went over to the breakfast nook table and sat down, pushing aside some of Mateo's papers to make space for his coffee mug. He looked intently at Mateo and waited. Nothing.

The silence was the worst of all. Simon coughed. Still no response from Mateo. He kicked his foot under the table, the first time hitting the leg of Mateo's chair, the second time driving his toes into Mateo's. "No 'good morning'? What? I don't merit that suddenly?"

Mateo leaned back in his chair and looked at Simon. "Morning," he said, cutthroat.

"That's a start." Simon sipped his coffee. The silence and the intent stares reminded him of their first date. Then, like now, his palms were sweaty, his stomach flipped, he searched for words and thought that nothing he said came out right. "Do you want to talk?"

"No."

"I do." Simon patted down the sides of his longish jet black hair. Mateo seemed to look at him dismissively, like he was nothing, useless. "If you want to talk, or if there's anything I can do —"

"I already said I don't want to talk," Mateo said. "If you want to do something, then … I want to be left alone." He focused his attention back on the manuscript pages spread out over the table.

"I'm not just one of your overzealous fans." Simon emphasized each word. "I'm your partner, your friend, as *you* said, your family." They weren't out in public where they sometimes had to dodge Mateo's fans hoping for an autograph or selfie. They didn't have to speak cryptically, check their emotions. "Stop pushing me away and talk to me."

Mateo, avoiding eye contact with Simon, collected his papers and left the kitchen.

Simon leaned forward, rested his elbows on the table and hid his face in his hands. He wanted to scream, scream so loud that it would shatter the china. *Would that be enough to wake him up, get him to confide in me again?* Simon sighed and a moment later strode into Mateo's office like a confident assassin determined to complete his mission. "What's wrong, Mateo?"

Mateo rooted through a desk drawer. "Nothing's wrong."

"You're acting like something's wrong, like —"

"You're not Dr. Phil and I'm not one of his celebrity nutcases." Mateo slammed the drawer closed. "Don't try to analyze me."

Simon didn't say a word. He was frustrated by how Mateo often insisted that he wasn't a celebrity. Oprah was a celebrity. The big J-C was a celebrity. Not Mateo, whose books sold by the millions. Mateo wasn't a big shot despite the fact that, during their five years together, he had been shortlisted twice for the Giller Prize and once for the Man Booker International Prize. But in that moment, Simon could see that Mateo was acting exactly like one of Dr. Phil's celebrity crackpots.

Simon sat down in the brown leather club chair in the corner where Mateo sometimes read. "I'm not sure if it's your father's death or Liam's return that has you the most upset. So why don't you tell me. Is it something I did? Are you angry at me for forcing you to go to the hospital?" He watched, his hands clenching and unclenching, as Mateo moved around the papers on his desk. "I mean, how could you never mention Liam?"

Mateo sat back in his chair, his eyes on fire and locked on Simon. "I need some time to digest everything that's happened in the last twenty-four hours. Do you get that?"

"Who is Liam? Is he your friend? Was he your lover?"

"Don't do this, Simon."

"Don't do what?"

"Make this all about you."

"I'm making this all about me?" Simon laughed grandly. "Yesterday, I watched Liam grope you, and you think I'm making this all about me?" There was a harshness in his voice that he couldn't push down. "Clearly, this is not about me. It's about you and whatever secrets you're keeping from me."

"Don't go there, Simon."

"Then tell me about Liam, who he is and what he means to you."

Mateo shrugged. "Liam's Zane and Melinda's friend from university. He doesn't mean anything to me."

"Do better." Simon scratched the deep runnel that ran from his upper lip to the base of his nose. "What's his connection to you?"

"There's no connection."

"There's something…" Simon's voice faltered, and he drew in a deep breath, knocking out his hostility. "If you're not friends, if you weren't lovers, what happened at the hospital —"

"Simon —"

"Just tell me, Mateo, so I stop imagining the worst. You know I've never kept secrets from you."

Mateo raised an eyebrow. "I don't think we want to have that conversation today."

"I just don't know how you couldn't mention him."

Mateo stood and stared out the window, his back to Simon. "Because before you and I met, Liam was no longer a part of my life. That was the choice he made."

"What does that mean?"

Mateo turned to face Simon. "It means that my friendship with Liam was complicated."

Simon's throat constricted. "So you are friends."

"I used the past tense."

"I'm not one of your students, either. I don't need a grammar lesson." Simon licked his lips. "Just friends?"

"Friends. Nothing more."

Why don't I believe him? Simon studied the man who had won his heart yet who, in that moment, he did not recognize. Simon had convinced himself that his and Mateo's relationship was built on total trust and brutal honesty, no matter what the cost. No secrets. No distorting of the truth. He had to believe that to steady the gaze of his own conscience. But there was something about Liam, about what was being left unsaid, that made Simon feel that a stranger had already succeeded at sidelining him. Or worse, that he had involuntarily released his claim on the most important person in his life.

Ding, dong, ding, dong. Simon and Mateo looked at each other and didn't move. The doorbell sounded again, and Mateo sat down at his desk. Simon gave Mateo a knowing glance and left to answer the door.

"I know it's early," Melinda said, barging into the house and dragging Zane by the hand behind her. "I wanted to stop by and see how you were holding up."

Simon closed the door. "Mateo doesn't want to talk about anything."

"Of course he doesn't," Melinda said, poking her head into the empty living room. "Is he —"

"In his office," Simon said.

Melinda's high heels thundered against the hardwood floor as she strutted down the hall.

Simon looked at Zane. "Too early for a drink?"

They laughed and went into the living room. Zane, seated on the sofa, looked about the room and pointed at the large painting with blue, black and white stripes on the far wall. "Is that new?"

"Yes." Simon lowered himself into the brown leather arm-chair. "We got it last week. I should say Mateo got it. He likes that abstract expressionism stuff. I don't get it though." He sat up straight, and crossed one leg over the other. "What's the deal with Liam?"

Zane scrunched his bushy eyebrows and then touched his right hand to his forehead, partly obscuring his view of Simon. He moved his hand away from his face and cleared his throat as he took in Simon's wild-eyed look. "I'm not sure what you mean."

"Is he a threat? Someone I should be concerned about? That he could come between Mateo and me?"

"Liam is, well…" Zane pursed his lips. How could he describe his best friend without making him out to be a sort of predator? "Liam is, I would say, unpredictable, but generally harmless."

"That's not very reassuring," Simon said askance.

"You heard first-hand his story about why he's back." Zane flicked his eyebrows. "You know as much as I do."

Simon drummed his fingers into the arm of the chair. "Do you believe him?"

"I have no reason to doubt him," Zane said quickly. "This is his home, where he grew up."

"It's just…" Simon uncrossed his legs. "Liam looked at Mateo the way, the way you look at someone you're in love with. The way you look at Melinda."

"Yes, I see your point." Zane fingered his goatee. "But what happened between Mateo and Liam was a long time ago."

"So something *did* happen." Simon fell back into his chair, disappointment twisted in his face.

Zane's eyes roved the room, avoiding Simon. After a few moments, he placed his left hand on the top of his head, which he tilted to the right. He held that position for about thirty seconds and then shifted his head to the left. It was a stretching exercise he'd always done before wrestling and it helped to calm his nerves. He completed ten sets. Then he began to shake his knee and whistle.

"What did you do, Zane?" Melinda said as she returned to the living room. She turned to Mateo, who stood beside her. "You know he only whistles when he's done something wrong and he knows it."

Zane bounced off the sofa and glanced at his watch. "Shouldn't we be heading over to your mother's?"

"I don't know what I'm going to do with him." Melinda gave Mateo a quick hug. "You and Simon should come. We're going to discuss the arrangements for Dad's funeral."

Mateo bristled. "You won't get me inside that house."

Melinda shook her head. "Stubborn like your father." She waved at Zane. "Come on. You know what Ryan will be like if we're late." She touched her hand to Mateo's arm. "I'll call you later." She smiled at Simon, who waved from the armchair.

The front door banged shut, and Simon went into the front hall. He and Mateo looked at each other the way two strangers do from across a crowded room, trying to deduce how they knew each other. Mateo shoved his hands in his pockets, Simon rubbed his nose and turned slightly away.

Simon, turning back towards Mateo, said, "Are you ever going to be honest with me about Liam?"

Mateo, staring blankly past Simon, looked tired and hurt.

Simon wondered if Mateo was thinking about Liam, fantasizing about him? "All right." Simon moved behind Mateo to grab the set of keys off the mahogany table. The front door swung open and closed with a bang.

Fifteen minutes later, Simon was holed up at Starbucks, nursing his blues over a grande soy latte.

2

ACROSS TOWN, LIAM SAT AT THE BAR-COUNTER IN HIS mother's kitchen, his hands loosely wrapped around the Snoopy-shaped mug that had survived his childhood. He stared blankly into the black liquid to avoid his mother's questioning look. But looking into that blackness made him nauseous, the blackness mirroring back to him the status of his life: nothingness. More than that. That some unnameable force that he had no power to fight against had stripped him, and his life, naked, and then defiled them both. Liam took a sip of his coffee and looked up. "Melinda's father died yesterday."

"I know," Susan said, wiping down the counter. "The CBC did a nice profile on him this morning and the work he did for the city. Such a loss."

"They're pretty shook up," Liam said.

"You know what it's like to lose a parent." Susan's eyes became moist. "It's devastating. And they'll have to grieve in public, and I've never thought that to be fair."

"Mr. Borden was on council a long time, wasn't he?"

Susan nodded. "Twenty years. Brought a lot of investment to the city. But most people remember him for his work with the homeless and getting the city to build more shelters and…" Susan froze. "Did you see him?"

"If you mean, Mateo, yes, I saw him."

"And?"

"Who do you think is more famous, Mateo or his father?"

Susan chucked the damp dish cloth at Liam, hitting him on the left side of his face. "That's not important. Did you talk to Mateo?"

Liam tossed the dish cloth back at his mother but missed, and it landed in the sink. "Yes. No. Not really. Not in the way that I had hoped. I mean, yesterday really wasn't the time." He sighed. "I don't know if he'll even talk to me again."

"You can't really blame him though," Susan said bluntly.

Liam briefly hid his face in his hands. "I don't need to be reminded of how I wronged him."

"I think you do." Susan made her way over to the end of the bar-counter and stood next to Liam with her arms folded. "You expected him, as young as he was, to drop everything and go with you. But it was all a shock, all so last-minute. So when he said no, you abandoned him, you cut him off. Over the years you came back to visit me and your father, and Zane and Melinda, and then to be with your father when he was ill, but you never saw Mateo, never reached out to him."

"I was humiliated."

"And rightly so. But you were also weak."

"I wasn't weak."

"Fine. You were an oaf."

"Mom!" A silence. "When's your next appointment with Doctor Reid?"

"Don't change the subject," Susan said. "I'm not blaming you —"

"It sounds like you are."

Susan sighed. "You need to try and see it from his perspective."

"There was nothing holding him here. And…" Liam shrugged. "What was stopping him from reaching out to me? I mean, if he really wanted to see me …" *But he did try … reaching out to me, that is. I was too humiliated and proud to respond. I was crushed. Later, I wasn't man enough to apologize so I did the only thing I knew how. I avoided him. Like he was a plague.*

Susan unfolded her arms and rubbed her right hand over Liam's broad back. "Maybe that's why you need to try to talk to Mateo again. Right? Find out —"

"I'm not sure. I don't know if it'll make a difference."

"Do you even know what you want from him?"

Liam gave a wry laugh. "No, not really." He looked at his mother, whose wide-open eyes carried her disbelief. "I guess I want us to be friends again."

"Friends or *friends*."

"Mom, he's with someone." Liam took a sip of his coffee. "And I'm pretty sure you didn't raise me to be a home wrecker."

They laughed.

Susan untied the strings of her apron, which she then folded and placed on the counter. "I promised your Aunt Hetty that I'd come over to the home this morning for a visit. I should be back by lunchtime if you need the car. And Dan called." As she went to leave the kitchen she stopped behind Liam and kissed the top of his head. "You know you have to talk to Mateo in a meaningful way." She left the kitchen, and a short time later slipped out the house, quietly closing the door behind her.

Liam stood, refilled his coffee mug, and made his way outside to the back deck. He sat down on one of the loungers, balancing his mug on his right thigh. What did he *really* want? A chance to go back in time, to undo the past, to have become a different man. For some time now he felt that he had let life get away from him, that he had ceded control to fate. How dastardly was that? Wasn't that what made him, to use his mother's term, weak?

The wind came up unexpectedly and knocked over the small, blue ceramic pot hosting the basil plant. The pot didn't break when it hit the veranda floor, but some of the earth spilled out and a couple of the basil plant leaves were crushed. Sprawled out on the deck floor, stems partly broken, that was how Liam felt when he first met Mateo all those years ago.

Liam was twenty-three and in his second year of law school. It was December, a week before Christmas, during the holiday social Zane and Melinda threw for their university friends. Mateo was there, as Melinda had put it, to look after Xavier, who was about twenty months old. Liam, when he first saw Mateo in the tiny yellow kitchen sneaking a glass of wine, elbowed Zane in the side and said, "Is that Mat … Mateo?"

"Yes." Zane rolled his eyes. "What's wrong with you?"

"Wow," Liam said under his breath. They weren't strangers, but Liam's sexual identity was in question, and now Mateo appeared different to him. Desirable. When Liam thought that no one was watching, he edged his way down the hall and into the small room that Zane and Melinda were using as a nursery.

Liam walked into the room without knocking. Mateo was seated in the white rocking chair reading, although Liam couldn't make out the title of the book. Mateo looked up, closed the book and lifted his index finger to his lips.

"I'm Liam," Liam said in a whisper, and held out his hand.

Mateo gripped Liam's clammy hand. "I know."

Liam chuckled. "So you're on babysitting duty?"

"I volunteered. Gets me out of the house. And Xavier's always good for me." Mateo gave Liam a wry look. "What are you doing here?"

Liam, surprised by Mateo's bluntness, stiffened. "It's a party —"

"I mean, what are you doing *here*, in this room?"

"Oh…" Liam, feeling two feet tall, shrugged. "Just thought I'd say hello. It didn't seem fair that you were holed up in here. It's a party…" He snapped his fingers as he swung his hands from side to side, gyrating his hips at the same time he rolled his head.

"Wow." Mateo raised his eyebrows. "What is that?"

"I'm dancing."

"Really? You call that dancing?"

Liam stopped moving. "Christ, I'm just … I was just trying to say that you should loosen up and enjoy this festive time."

"You suck."

"God, do I ever."

Mateo laughed.

Liam walked over to the crib and stared at Xavier, who lay there absolutely still, and it didn't seem like he was even breathing. Liam was relieved when Xavier's tiny fingers curled slightly. "What are you reading?"

"*Wuthering Heights.*"

"Christ!"

"It's on the reading list for my English class, and I'm writing a paper on it next semester."

"Next semester?" Liam shook his head. "Aren't you in high school?"

"First-year university." Mateo was seventeen.

"But…" Liam scrunched his eyebrows. "You're —"

"Brilliant." Mateo laughed. "I skipped a grade."

"And is this what you do for fun? Babysit your nephew?"

"I also run."

"We should go for a run together sometime."

"Why?"

"Sometimes it's nice to run with someone."

"Aren't you crazy busy with law school? Zane's crazy busy —"

"Maybe I'm brilliant, too." Liam bit down on his lower lip. "How did you know I was in law school?"

Mateo rolled his eyes. "Zane's friends are all stuck-up, hoity-toity law students."

"Well, I'm pretty chill," Liam said, hoping he sounded cool.

"Maybe. But I think you're too old for me to be hanging out with."

"You certainly don't have your sister's charm," Liam said.

"I don't have her boobs, either."

Liam's eyes narrowed. "Why the attitude?"

"Why are you still *here*?"

"Right…" Liam drawled, and looked on, defeated, as Mateo opened his book and continued reading. Liam stood there a moment longer and then left the room.

There was another surge of wind that rolled the pot with the basil plant towards the veranda steps. The pot stopped short of the edge. Liam was back at the edge, unsure if he had tumbled over the cliff or remained standing. *I've always let him make me feel weak, ever since the beginning.* He gulped his cold coffee. He was never sure how to proceed with Mateo, then or now. Then there had been something intriguing about Mateo that Liam was desperate to discover. Seeing Mateo again now, after such a long absence, left him aching to uncover that something intriguing. He had persisted back then with Mateo and they had somehow managed to become friends. It might have helped, too, that when they had met Liam was still playing at being straight and was engaged, briefly, to a girl named Lisbeth Hall. Maybe he wasn't that much of a threat.

Liam set his half-full mug of coffee down on the floor of the deck and moved to clean up the mess from the upended basil plant. When that was done, he returned to the lounger, stared up into the sky, the blue expanse dotted with light white fluffy clouds, and felt empty. More than empty. He felt dead. Mateo was the only person Liam had ever loved in an authentic way, but he never succeeded at executing that love, proving its worth. Was it too late? He was miserable and lost and unloved. He closed his eyes and breathed deeply. A man who was somewhat skeptical of faith, Liam offered the following silent prayer, "Lord, guide me, hold me, lead me in the direction of Your will. Help me to know and trust Thy word. Give me a sign so that I may know what I should do. Amen."

3

"LET US —"

"Don't say pray," Melinda said, waving her hand at Ryan. "I think there's been enough praying for one day." She turned to her mother, who was seated in the blue and white striped wingback chair where her father used to read the paper. "Is there anything special Dad wanted in terms of his funeral service?"

Doris, her eyes filled with tears, shook her head. She opened her mouth to speak but words failed her. She dropped her head and, as she had done for most of the time since Melinda and Zane had arrived at the house, cried. Her tears had removed most of her makeup, revealing a few deep lines in her round, toffee-coloured face. She looked tired, lost, devastated, and Melinda, trying not to be dogmatic about grieving, struggled to hide her annoyance at her mother's fragility. Now was the time to make decisions, to get things done. They could grieve after the funeral, in private.

"Well, naturally," Ryan said, "I'll give Dad's eulogy," and looked about the room for confirmation.

"Why, 'naturally?'" Melinda asked.

"Because I'm the eldest, and the minister —"

"But is that what Dad wanted?" Melinda sighed frustration at the silence. *Lord, come now into this house and slap these people awake.*

Zane, who was holed up in the kitchen, came into the living room as voices grew louder. He had spotted a pile of envelopes on the edge of the counter and grabbed them before leaving the kitchen. Once in the living room he waved the envelopes in the air. "What are these?"

"Those are none of your business," Ryan said, and charged towards Zane.

Zane held the envelopes high above his head and rolled his eyes as Ryan jumped up in the air trying to snatch them away. After sidestepping Ryan, Zane began to distribute the envelopes. There was one for Melinda, Benjamin and Mateo. Zane handed Mateo's envelope to Melinda, who immediately tore open her own. It contained a letter penned by her father that brought tears to her eyes.

Benjamin, standing in front of the living room window, handed his letter to Betty, who read it quickly. He waited for Betty to hand it back and then said, "Dad wants Mateo to give his eulogy?"

"He has no right," Ryan said.

"He has every right," Melinda said as she folded her letter and slipped it back into the envelope. "If that's what Dad wanted —"

"Well, he's not giving it. I am." Ryan pointed at his chest. "That's my right. I've earned it."

"Stop it!" Doris said, and wiped her face with a well-used tissue but the tears still flowed. "This is not how your father would want you to act." She breathed deeply, her large bosom rising and falling. "Let's try to remain calm and think this through." She took a moment to study each of her children's faces, and she could see a little bit of Peter in each of them. "As much as possible I will respect your father's last wishes, but … Ryan's right. Mateo shouldn't be allowed to give the eulogy. He's not part of —"

"Mama!" Melinda fell back into the sofa and cupped her hands to the sides of her head. She wanted to scream. She didn't consider herself to be superstitious, but she was certain that nothing good could come of denying a dead man's last wish. She pulled her hands away from the sides of her head, brought herself forward and clasped her hands together, resting them on her lap. She gave her mother a hard, disapproving look. "First off, Mateo *is* part of this family. And if he isn't, well, whose fault is that?" She was unmoved by her mother's critical, wide-eyed knotted face. "Second, there's nothing to think through. We're going to put aside whatever childish issues we have and try to, at least, honour Dad's final request. I'll talk to Mateo."

"It's not your decision, Melinda," Ryan said.

Melinda pointed her left index finger at Ryan. "You're right. It's not yours, either. It was Dad's. Like I said, I'll talk to Mateo."

"Actually…" Benjamin pushed his pursed lips from side to side. "In his letter Dad asked me to do that." He stared intently at Melinda. "I'll at least give it a try."

"I'm pretty sure that Peter already planned out his funeral," Zane said. "He had mentioned something along those lines to me after his last heart attack. If you…" He stopped to let out a belch and, without excusing himself, continued. "Check the file with his will. He probably put whatever instructions he left in that."

"That would certainly settle everything." Melinda bounced off the sofa. "I'll check Dad's office." She went to leave the room and, as she passed by Zane, reached out for his hand. She squeezed it and rushed down the hall.

"Now, hold on," Ryan said as he chased after Melinda.

A silence settled over the living room. No one looked at each other. They listened to Melinda and Ryan, shouting at the other end of the house. They couldn't make out everything. But the few expletives, used by Melinda, came through loud and clear. That made Doris twitch.

Melinda reappeared in the living room, waving a piece of paper. "Here it is. Just like Zane said." She read from the piece of paper, in Peter's scrawling handwriting, how he had envisioned his funeral service unfolding. She walked around the room afterwards, showing the outline to everyone. Next to *Eulogy* was Mateo's name, but her thumb intentionally covered up the question mark next to it. "There's nothing to think about. It's both here and in the letter. Dad's wishes are here in black and white." She folded the paper and slid it through the V-neck opening of her dress, secure against her right breast. "And when are we meeting with the funeral home people?"

"I'm meeting with them at two," Ryan said.

"We should all go," Melinda said, now taking charge of the situation.

"That's not necessary," Ryan said, his prominent nostrils flaring. "I'll handle it."

"We'll all go," Melinda said with emphasis. As Ryan was about to speak, she raised her hand in the air.

Ryan, shaking and his face tied up in knots, stormed out of the room, his wife Carole quick to go after him.

Melinda looked at her watch. Twelve thirty. "Let's all get a quick bite to eat." Looking at Benjamin, she said, "Zane and I will drop you off at Mateo's after the meeting at the funeral home." Everyone remained still until Melinda stomped her right foot and clapped her hands as if herding cattle. "Move, people! We haven't got all day!"

The room cleared out, and Zane went over to Melinda and wrapped his arms around her waist. "God, you're hot when you're bossy," and went to cover her mouth with his.

Melinda shoved him away and shook her right fist at him. "What's that smell?"

Zane smirked. "Vodka. Grey Goose, actually. From your father's private stash."

"If Mama —"

"Doris knew about it. She felt better pretending like your father didn't drink. And you know he could drink me under the table."

"Regardless…" Melinda stood with her hands on her hips. "I ought to kick that skinny white ass of yours to the moon. Really, you shouldn't be drinking at this hour of the day."

"I'm toasting your father," Zane said. "He wouldn't want that vodka to go to waste."

"If you don't cut it out and sober up, we'll be toasting you, too."

Zane stuck out his tongue, then winked.

Melinda tried to keep a straight face, but her lips spread into a thin smile. Zane always made her laugh when she needed to the most. She touched her hand to his shoulder. *I might just make it through this day after all*. She moved off, joining the others in the kitchen.

4

Simon Denault gulped the last mouthful of his soy
latte. It was actually his fourth drink since he had arrived at
the Starbucks on Spring Garden Road. His mind was still in
tumult, and he didn't want to return home without some type
of plan. He needed to know about Mateo's past and the role
Liam Robertson had played. He wasn't naïve. He knew Mateo had had other relationships before him. But to not mention Liam, who had a strong connection to the Borden family, made him nervous. *He's not telling me everything. Why?
What's the big secret?* Liam's presence created uncertainty,
and for the first time in five years the possibility of losing
Mateo felt very real to Simon. The unknown nurtured his fear,
made him woozy. He couldn't lose Mateo, not when he had
lost so much already.

Simon had purposely cut himself off from his family, a
self-imposed exile. He grew up in Brossard, on the outskirts
of Montréal, and was the eldest of three. He was a quiet child
and kept to himself. Once he learned to read his nose was
always in a book, eager to discover a world far greater than
the one he inhabited. His determination to learn English,
which had been banned in the family home, disappointed his
parents, who were well-known in the Quebec independence
movement. Yet it was his indifference to the cause that broke

their hearts. And in Pierre-Luc Denault's house politics meant more than religion. Simon's federalist leanings were beyond treasonous. They were sacrilege. His father looked at him like he was dead, like he no longer existed.

He told himself that it would be better for his family for him to leave once he was able. His only way out was university. An exceptional student, every university Simon applied to offered him a full scholarship. His decision to attend the University of Toronto, an English institution in enemy territory, was the final nail in the coffin. He hadn't spoken to his father since. How could Simon turn his back on his family, his culture, his *patrimoine*? And so he fled — first to Toronto and then to Ottawa, where he completed his master's degree and then onto Halifax for his doctoral studies. He had never expected to stay in Halifax and often thought about returning to Toronto or Ottawa. But he started teaching, started climbing the academic ladder, and slowly began to build a life for himself.

Simon knew that leaving his family had made all the difference. He was, after all, following his own path, which was what his father espoused for Quebec. But to his father he was more than a traitor because he had never picked a side. Traitors picked a side, waged a war for what they believed in. Simon tried to remain neutral, to stay out of the fray.

Over the years, the time apart gave both men a chance to think, to see what really mattered. His father's phone call on his thirty-second birthday had shocked. Conversation didn't come easy, but the call ended with an invitation for Simon to come home. He went. He remembered most of all his father's teary eyes and the heartfelt, "*À la prochaine fois*," at the airport after an unexpected hug. What really mattered, to both of them, was family — too important to cast aside and deserving of a second chance.

The day Simon had met Mateo, he had just returned from his first trip back "home" to Brossard since he had left for university. He had created a family for himself through his friends from university. So it had felt odd to, during the visit, come out to his parents. They weren't shocked. It didn't seem to matter at all. They were so happy to have their son back, to know that they hadn't lost him completely.

While he now had a better relationship with his parents, Simon wasn't ready to go through that type of loss again. Time had strained his relationship with his university friends as they had all settled down, followed their dreams that took them to different parts of the country. They tried to stay connected through e-mail and Facebook, but their lives were busy and full. As Simon was to Mateo, Mateo was Simon's family, his refuge. He had given his all to Mateo, to *them*, and he wasn't about to be pushed aside by some ghost from the past. Liam wasn't a ghost, but he was from the past, and Simon was determined to keep Liam there, in Mateo's past.

Simon made for the exit, tossing the empty paper cup in the garbage on his way. He walked determinedly towards his and Mateo's Bridges Street home. He and Mateo were going to *talk*, clear the air. Necessary things would be said, where truth and honesty had dominion, and they would end up closer, their love stronger, and their future together assured.

5

AFTER LEAVING MEMORIAL FUNERAL HOME, MELINDA dropped Zane off in front of the blue house on Flinn Street. Ten minutes later, she brought her silver Jetta to a stop in front of Mateo's Bridges Street home. She and Betty bounced out of the car and waited for Benjamin, who seemed to hesitate with each of his movements. Melinda saw the doubt already building in Benjamin's eyes as he neared, like this wasn't the right play. Benjamin took Betty's hand in his and stood there at the bottom of the driveway. Melinda rolled her eyes and said, "We haven't got all day," and guided them towards the house. Standing on the front porch, Benjamin again just stood there. Melinda poked him in the back but there was no reaction. "For the love of God." She reached between Betty and Benjamin, and rang the doorbell. As they waited, she leaned into Benjamin's ear and said, "I don't know who cut off your balls, but you better find them and sew them back on before we step into that house."

There was the sound of the deadbolt turning over, after which the door opened wide and they were greeted by a shocked-looking Mateo who, after a moment, said, "Come in." He closed the door, and it was as if some type of spell had been cast. They stood there sporting quirky smiles that made them all look a bit crazy, and awkward, and they diverted their eyes every time their gazes met.

"Oh, this is silly," Melinda said, and flung her arms in the air. "Mateo, do you have any of that Australian merlot Simon keeps on hand? I'd love a glass. Wouldn't you, Betty?"

Betty could feel the heat rushing into her cheeks, and moved her narrow green eyes from Benjamin, then to Mateo and finally Melinda. She reached behind her head and pulled her long brown hair over her shoulder. "Well, I … I wouldn't want to inconvenience —"

"It's not an inconvenience," Melinda said, her gaze focused on Mateo. "Is it…"

Mateo looked coolly at Melinda for a moment, rolled his eyes and disappeared down the short hall and into the kitchen.

Melinda shepherded Benjamin and Betty into the living room and, after assuring them that everything was fine, went into the kitchen where she found Mateo standing in front of the sink and staring out the window. She tapped her long, red-painted fingernails against the countertop but Mateo didn't flinch. "Matté!"

Mateo spun around. "Don't call me that."

"You never used to mind when Li —"

"I mind now." Mateo reached for the bottle of merlot that he had retrieved from the wine rack before Melinda appeared and unscrewed the cap. "So what's this? Some type of intervention?"

"You know, Matté, I've never been a fan of your sarcasm."

"I said don't call me that." He poured out three glasses of wine. "Then what is it? Why are they here?"

"Because they're family." Melinda took a glass of wine and tasted it. "And Benjamin needs to talk to you."

"About what?"

"Dad's funeral."

Mateo shook his head. "No, no way. Not today. It's the last thing I need." He screwed the cap back on the wine bottle and folded his arms. "Your husband has a big mouth."

"What are you talking about?" Melinda, without realizing it, was halfway through her glass of wine. She had to slow down. Drinking made her petulant.

"He said something to Simon about Liam and me. I don't know exactly what he said, but now Simon is pissed. He stormed out of here this morning after your visit and he's not answering his phone."

"What's the big deal? Liam's one of your closest friends."

"Was," Mateo said. "Liam *was* my closest friend, my best friend." He massaged his temple with his hand. "I never told Simon about Liam."

Melinda choked on her mouthful of wine, and placed the wineglass on the counter as she coughed. She held her hand to her chest and looked quizzically at Mateo. "You never told Simon about Liam? How could you not? I mean —"

"What was I supposed to say?"

"Now it's about what you didn't say with Liam being back." Melinda picked up her wineglass and another one. "But don't blame Zane. It's not his fault. And don't blame Simon, either. He has every right to be scared given your history with Liam."

"Melinda, don't be absurd."

"Then why didn't you tell Simon about Liam?" She gave him that motherly, I-told-you-so look. "That's what I thought. But I don't have the time or the patience to solve your Liam problem. You can deal with that later. Like I said, Benjamin needs to talk to you."

"Melinda, I —"

"This isn't KFC. Did you hear me give you choices off a menu?" Melinda pointed at the third glass of wine. "Pick up the glass of wine and come talk to your brother." She stomped her foot when Mateo didn't move. "And stop acting like a … a goddamn prick."

Mateo took a moment to breathe, to shake off the rage running though his veins and set to burst. Melinda's words had struck a nerve, made him think about old feelings, un-explored possibilities. But that didn't mean that his life with Simon was in danger. Or did it? He was no longer sure, and that frightened him. That had to wait. He had to deal with Benjamin, and that set his rage bubbling again and he wasn't sure he could tamp it down. He picked up the remaining wine-glass and headed for the living room. Benjamin and Betty were seated on the sofa, Melinda in one of the armchairs. Mateo, his eyes scanning the room, handed the wineglass to Benjamin and, ignoring Melinda's gesture to sit down in the armchair next to her, remained standing.

"It's a lovely home," Betty said timidly, hoping to break the awkward silence.

"Thanks." Mateo smiled faintly. Betty reminded him of someone with her long straight nose and thin lips. She didn't wear a lot of makeup, but was pretty and confident about her looks.

"It's nice to finally meet you," Betty said, and sipped her wine. "There wasn't really an opportunity at the hospital."

Melinda bolted upright in her chair. "You two aren't meeting for the first time, are you?"

Betty glanced at Benjamin, who dropped his head. "Well, yes…"

"Don't act so surprised by that," Mateo said to Melinda. "We weren't all invited to the gathering welcoming Betty into the family. You *know* that."

"Like you would have come," Benjamin said under his breath but everyone heard it.

"You're the one who left, cut yourself off," Mateo said, his voice elevated. "You're absolutely right. I wouldn't have gone to meet a total stranger's wife."

"Stop it!" Melinda set her wineglass down on the coffee table. "We didn't come here to debate the past."

Benjamin looked up at Mateo. "You know what it means to cut yourself off. When Mama closed the door on you, you assumed that everyone was against you. You never dared to think that I wouldn't care who you fucked."

"Benjamin!" Melinda shouted. "There's no need for that type of language."

Betty reached for Benjamin's hand and held it tightly.

"How could I know if you cared or didn't care?" Mateo placed his hands on the back of the vacant armchair. "It's not like you ever called."

"Don't put that shit on me." Benjamin bounced off the sofa, violently shaking his hand free of Betty's grasp, and looked as if he was about to rush Mateo. "For once in your life stop blaming everyone for your screw-ups. Shit happens. So don't make me your fucking Judas." He waved off Melinda's disapproving look. "You know what it was like growing up in that house, with *her*. You weren't the only one who had issues with Mama. I left home to get away from her, from her trying to control me. Just like you did. The only difference is that you moved across the city while I left the province."

Mateo threw Benjamin a mocking look, but he knew exactly what Benjamin meant. Their mother used the Bible as a whip to hold them in check, keep them "on the straight and narrow." Benjamin was already in Toronto when Melinda's pregnancy set off an atom bomb in the Borden house. His mother exploded at breakfast into a tirade about the black man's plight and how Melinda's carelessness wasn't helping the cause. The lunchtime detonation focused on Satan and the evil ways of the world. The suppertime blow-up came after dessert, about choosing to be a soldier of the cross or a man of the world. The explosions continued daily until Melinda fled and moved in with Zane out of wedlock. Another ungodly act. With Melinda out of the house, Doris was determined to keep Mateo out of Satan's reach — enacting her own version of the War Measures Act, trying to control where he went, when and with whom. Melinda's teen pregnancy was the beginning of an insurrection, and Doris was not about to let Mateo join the jihad.

Betty and Melinda were exchanging doubting looks when the front door swooshed open. Simon, sporting a frenzied look and clearly dismayed by the presence of the others in the living room, was hesitant to enter the room. He felt the tension that everyone was wrapped up in, and it was slowly taking over him. Simon said, "What's going on?"

"Nothing," Mateo said sharply. "They were just leaving."

"No, we weren't." Melinda stood and walked across the room and hugged Simon. Pushing away from him, she turned back into the room and pointed at Benjamin and Mateo. "I need these two to talk. It's important."

Simon came into the living room and, when he couldn't catch Mateo's eye, shrugged. "I don't think I can help with that."

"Yes, you can." Melinda went to collect her wineglass and held her hand out to Betty. "You can show Betty the house." When Betty stood and had taken her hand, Melinda said, "Wait until you see the en suite in the master bedroom. It's divine." She led Betty out of the living room and into the front hall.

Benjamin, Mateo and Simon stood there, immured in silence, eyes roving the room. There was a disconnect that no one seemed eager to fix. Benjamin sat back down on the sofa, his eyes glued to the floor as he sipped his wine. Mateo looked dismissively at Simon, who shoved his hands in his pockets and left the room.

After Simon had disappeared, Mateo moved in front of the living room window and watched as the kids across the street played basketball in their driveway. Could he and Benjamin find a way to speak to each other and were they willing to try? Or were they too wrapped up in the past and the misunderstandings that separated them?

Benjamin said, "I didn't mean to shout," and looked up. The silence lingered, and he ran his hand over his face. "I'm not your enemy, Mateo. You may not believe that but it's true." He gulped the last mouthful of his wine and set his wineglass on the coffee table. "Betty and I dated during our last year of high school. Her father was against me because I'm black, and Mama was against Betty because she's white. It was like the 1960s were alive all over again. Black had to stay with black, white with white. I didn't want to play that game so, yes, I left. Betty was planning on studying in Toronto too until her father realized why that was." He sat back in the sofa. "We kept in touch, tried to hang on to each other. That wasn't easy given the distance. But when Betty's father died, she came to Toronto and we started dating again. I don't know why we waited so long to get married. Well, I didn't want Mama going off again. You know how Melinda marrying Zane sent Mama into a tizzy. Or maybe we were expecting Betty's father to rise up from the dead." He gave a wry laugh. "I mean, Melinda and Zane, me and Betty, you and Simon … Mama must be wondering what she did to drive us to the white side."

"We sure didn't keep the family pure," Mateo said with a hint of sarcasm and spun around. "At the hospital Doris did seem cordial enough with Betty."

"Mama's great at playing cordial," Benjamin said. "It seems like she's accepted Betty, but I'm never really sure." He ran his tongue across his upper lip. "How do you get away with calling her Doris?"

"Until yesterday I hadn't seen her in nine years. I don't think of her as my mother. Doris seems like the right moniker. It's her name after all." Mateo, moving hesitantly about the room, eventually sat down in the armchair that Melinda had occupied earlier. He tried to study his brother discreetly, but each time he went to look at Benjamin their eyes met, and Mateo would look away. Benjamin was about an inch shorter than Mateo, and was slender like his younger brother. He kept his hair cut very close, but not shaved off like Mateo's. *What does he want?* Mateo lifted his gaze. "So how long should we do this?"

"Do what?" Benjamin asked.

Mateo grimaced, leaned back in his chair and crossed his left leg over his right. "What do you want?"

"For the sweet fucking love of God, Mateo…" Benjamin brought himself forward to the edge of the sofa and clasped his hands together. "I'm trying to make peace here. And it's about Dad's funeral —"

"Don't involve me in that," Mateo said, curt.

"You're already involved," Benjamin shot back. "Dad involved you, with his letters."

"What letters?"

"Oh, right…" Benjamin stood and went into the front hall and bellowed, "Melinda!" Almost immediately Melinda came into view, and Benjamin said to her, "Can you give Mateo his letter?"

"Oh, of course," Melinda said, and hurried into the living room to retrieve her red purse. She pulled out the envelope with Mateo's name on it and handed it to him. "Dad left a letter for each of us."

Mateo tossed the letter onto the coffee table. "Look," he said priggishly and stood. "Do whatever you want for Peter's funeral. I don't care."

"You should care," Melinda said, raising her voice. "He was your father and he loved you. That's why he wants you to give his eulogy."

Mateo burst out laughing. "Don't be ridiculous," he said after he calmed down.

Benjamin came back into the room and stood next to Melinda. "Read your letter. He mentioned that request to all of us in each letter."

Mateo sighed, reached for his envelope and tore it open. He pulled out the letter, unfolded it and his eyes danced across the pages. He gave a nervous laugh and looked questioningly at Benjamin and Melinda. "Is this supposed to be some colossal joke?"

Melinda reached out for Mateo's hand. "You've got to do this. If Ryan gets his way —"

"He'll portray Dad like the great messiah," Benjamin cut in. "Dad made mistakes. He was human. I think his wish for you to give his eulogy was his way of acknowledging those mistakes."

Mateo let go of Melinda's hand and, still clutching the letter, fell down into the armchair as if he had fainted. "And what would I say? Let me tell you about Peter Borden, the father who wasn't much of a father to me?"

"Mateo!" Melinda folded her arms. "Don't be like that."

Mateo, taking a moment to again scan the letter's contents, looked up at Benjamin. "And so Peter wanted you to sell this to me?"

Benjamin nodded. "He wanted us to find a way to talk to each other. I think he knew we could be allies."

"This is too much." Mateo set the letter back down on the coffee table and stood. "I need to get some air." He strode across the living room and into the front hall, where he stabbed his feet into his shoes and, without his wallet or keys, left the house.

AT THE LOUD THUD OF THE FRONT DOOR BANGING SHUT Betty and Simon, leaving Simon's office at the end of the hall, charged towards the living room.

"What happened?" Simon asked, his heart racing.

"We're trying to organize Dad's funeral," Benjamin said.

"And Mateo, as usual, is being difficult," Melinda said. She slung the strap of her purse over her right shoulder and pointed at Simon. "You need to talk to him. He'll listen to you." She looked at her watch and turned to Benjamin and Betty. "I should get you two back to Mama's. I've got to pick up Zane and then get home to Xavier."

Everyone made their way to the front hall where hugs and handshakes were exchanged.

"Sorry about the intrusion," Benjamin said to Simon. He opened the door and led Betty by the hand out of the house.

Melinda stayed behind a moment. "He loves you. You shouldn't doubt that." When Simon dropped his gaze, Melinda added, "I know Mateo didn't tell you about Liam. That was his way of coping. Liam hurt him in a real, deep way."

"Yet Mateo and Liam never dated," Simon said with disbelief.

"It's not what you're thinking." Melinda looped her arm through Simon's. "Liam being back is a shock. Be patient. Give Mateo time to digest the shock. Then he'll tell you what happened, but it's not my place, or anyone else's, to tell you about that." She tugged on Simon's arm and they walked together to her car. Melinda climbed in and flipped the engine. She lowered the driver's side window and, shifting the car into drive, said, "Please talk to Mateo about Dad's funeral. Try to talk some sense into him."

Simon wasn't convinced that he could talk to Mateo, or that Mateo would listen. "I'll try." He waved as the car rolled down the street.

6

Zane was across town at Susan Robertson's house. He was in Liam's office with the door closed. Zane stood in front of the desk, a beer bottle clutched in his hand, and studied the collection of certificates, diplomas and awards hanging on the wall. Then he shifted his gaze to Liam, who was seated behind his desk with disillusionment etched in his face. Zane broke the silence with, "You majored in English?"

"Yes." Liam, leaning back in the desk chair, brought himself forward. The disdain in Zane's voice had caught him off guard. Or was it disbelief? "I told you that when we first met."

"I guess." Zane gulped his beer, pulled out the wooden chair that was up against the wall and sat down. "Did you ever want to write? Like Mateo?"

"I tried, but not very hard." Liam smirked. "I was too afraid of failing, of never making it. Then again, maybe I never had the courage to keep at it." He fixed his gaze on Zane, who was staring intently at him. "What?"

"You tell me." Zane set his near-empty beer bottle down on the desk with a loud clank. "What are you doing back here? And don't try to sell that cockamamie story about coming back to look after you mother. I didn't buy that at the hospital, not like Melinda. You and I both know you're not that much of a saint."

"Well, it's partly true," Liam said, going on the defensive. "I want to be here for my mother. Now she's in remission but if she ends up sick again there's no one here to help her. You never met my sister, Cassandra. She lives in Winnipeg and, as a Jehovah Witness, well … I can't imagine her being helpful if Mom ever needed a blood transfusion. What if I weren't there but my sister was, and Mom couldn't speak for herself. Would Cassandra withhold consent?" He sighed. "That's why I need to be here. My mother doesn't have anyone else."

Zane sat up straight. "What happened in New York?"

"Nothing happened in New York," Liam said, pained. "I couldn't get grounded there, couldn't anchor myself. All I did was work. Everyone kept saying that I had to put in my time, pay my dues, but in eight years nothing changed, except my salary. What's the point of making lots of money if you can't enjoy it?"

"What about Mateo?"

"What about him?"

"I know how you felt about him when you left. Has that changed? Again, I'm not Melinda, so don't try to bullshit me."

Liam shot out of his chair and stood with his hands cupped to the back of his head. "He's the only man I've ever loved."

"Oh, Liam, Christ!" Zane fell back in his chair and sucked his teeth. "So now what? Are you going to make a play for him? Find a way to get Simon out of the way?"

"Don't, Zane." Liam's hands dropped to his sides. "I would never —"

"All right. Sit down and stop being so sentimental." Zane reached for his beer bottle and gulped it until it was gone. "So

Mateo is the only man you've loved. But he's happy, with Simon."

"If you're worried about this being some kind of fatal attraction, don't." Liam shook his head. "I'm not *that* crazy about him. I just..." He bit down on his lower lip. "I want to do things differently now. I want to do something inspiring, be around inspiring people."

"Oh, gee, shucks," Zane said, chuckling.

Liam groaned. "You don't inspire me."

They laughed.

"What's your game plan?" Zane asked.

Liam shrugged. "Buy a place and get settled."

"I'm talking about Mateo."

"I simply want to talk to him and try to apologize."

"Just talk?"

"Yes, just talk." Liam sounded exasperated. "I don't know why it is that you and my mother think I'm some kind of male jezebel."

"Well, there was that guy —"

"Oh, fuck off!" Liam, breathing deeply, sat back down behind the desk. "All I know is that I have to do something different with my life now. I just don't have a fucking clue as to what that is."

"You can start by getting a job," Zane said, matter-of-fact. "You have too much time on your hands, too much time to brood."

"And do what?" Liam looked defeated.

"Maybe you need to try a different approach," Zane said. "Instead of being a cog in one of those large full-service law firms, maybe you should consider going out on your own. You know, set up your own practice."

"I'm thinking about giving up law."

"Now you're talking nonsense." Zane ran his hand over his head. "Maybe you should see someone, like a psychologist."

"I'm not crazy."

"Maybe there's some type of imbalance —"

"Zane, I'm not crazy," Liam said, almost shouting. "I may be in love with a guy I know I can't be with, but that doesn't make me crazy."

"It makes you stupid," Zane said in a barely audible voice.

"What?"

"I said it makes you stupid," Zane blurted out. "I'm sorry. I didn't mean that."

"You've never said anything to me that you didn't mean." After a long silence, Liam stood. "Maybe you should go."

"Oh…" Zane licked his lips, hesitated, then rose to his feet. "Look, Liam, if there's anything I can do —"

Liam waved Zane off and moved to the door, which he opened and waited on Zane to leave the room. It was a short distance from Liam's office to the front door where they looked searchingly at each other. "I don't expect you to understand this —"

"I can't understand it," Zane interrupted. "You haven't explained much of anything." He took a step forward and cupped his hands to Liam's shoulders. "But I'm your best friend, and I'll support you however I can. Do you want me to call a couple of people I know at some of the other law firms and see if there are any openings?"

"No." Liam wiggled out of Zane's grasp and moved to open the front door.

"If you need anything, or want to talk —"

"Zane, I'll be fine. Really."

Zane headed towards the door, and he was about to cross over the threshold when he turned around to look at Liam. "Mateo's not the same guy you walked out on. And now he's angry. Maybe at you, or maybe at the whole world…" Zane censored himself. He could see the disinterest in Liam's lifeless eyes. He nodded and left the house.

7

Simon busied himself in the kitchen. He unloaded and loaded the dishwasher. Scrubbed the backsplash. Refolded the dish towels and dish cloths. Arranged the spice jars alphabetically. Mopped the floor. He was trying to re-establish a sense of order, unravel himself from the chaos swirling about him. But none of that helped. Order would only be restored when he and Mateo talked, took down the barriers. When they were willing to, one more time, trust each other.

Putting the mop and bucket away, Simon's heart leapt into his throat when he heard the front door swoosh open. He rushed out of the kitchen and into the foyer. Mateo, stepping out of his shoes, had his back to him. *This is it. We have to talk. The silence has got to end.* Simon shoved his hands in his pockets and waited. Mateo spun around and their eyes locked. They looked warily at each other and sensed that something had shifted between them. It was too early to say if the shift was permanent, or how they would be affected by it.

"Are you hungry?" Simon asked.

"Not really," Mateo said.

"When was the last time you ate something?"

At Mateo's languid shrug, Simon pulled his hands out of his pockets and reached for Mateo's hands and held them. Walking backwards, he guided Mateo into the kitchen and forced him to sit down at the breakfast nook table. He went to the fridge and took out the plate, wrapped down in cellophane, which had the chicken salad sandwich he had made in between unloading the dishwasher and scrubbing the backsplash. He tore off the cellophane as he walked back to the table and set the plate down in front of Mateo. He crumpled the plastic wrap into a ball and chucked it onto the counter, and poured out two glasses of red wine before joining Mateo at the table.

Mateo picked up the sandwich, took a bite and chewed thoughtfully while his eyes averted Simon's gaze. "Thanks," he said and took another bite.

Simon sipped his wine. "I know … I shouldn't have … I read the letter your father wrote to you."

Mateo swallowed his mouthful of food. "I see."

"I didn't mean to, but it was there on the coffee table and…" Simon paused, and continued with, "I'm sorry I did that."

"No, you're not."

"No, I'm not," Simon said pointedly. "It was the only way for me to figure out what's going on since you won't talk to me." Simon reached across the table and tried to place his hand on Mateo's arm but Mateo jerked his arm away. "I don't know what I've done, why you've cut me out." He curled his fingers into fists as Mateo sat silent. "Mateo, you need to talk to me."

"And say what?" Mateo glared menacingly at Simon. "All I want is to be left alone. Why is that so fucking hard for everyone to understand?"

The harshness in Mateo's voice, the vulgarity, forced Simon to look down. Mateo had never spoken to him like that, which now had him on the verge of tears. He pushed back his chair, stood, picked up his wineglass and stormed out of the kitchen. He took refuge in the living room, sat on the sofa and tried not to cry. Everything was falling apart and he didn't understand what was happening, or the role he may have played. Yet he was desperate to find a way to put it all back together, as if that was his duty and, perhaps, his only redeeming act.

The only thing Simon was certain of was that Liam was to blame for everything that was happening. Liam's return had unsettled everything, created a wedge between them that wouldn't move, couldn't be extracted. What was it about Liam that was so mesmerizing? What happened between Mateo and Liam and why was it such a secret? *I need to know what happened between them. Otherwise, we don't stand a chance, we won't survive this.* He gulped back his wine like it was grape juice and let out a loud belch. He caught a glimpse of Mateo, who had quietly entered the room and was standing just inside the entryway. His heart thumped in his chest.

"I'm sorry for how I spoke to you," Mateo said, and went to sit down in one of the armchairs. Seated, he sipped his wine and looked at Simon. "You didn't deserve that."

"No, I didn't."

"I just…" Mateo stared abstractly at the floor. "I can't think straight."

"So you're taking that out on me?"

"Not intentionally."

"It feels intentional." Simon stood and left the room. He returned a few moments later with a full glass of wine and the wine bottle, and topped up Mateo's glass. "I want to help," he said, setting the half-full wine bottle on the coffee table and then taking up his earlier position on the sofa. "What are you going to do about your father's funeral?"

"Nothing."

"Mateo!" Simon moved off the sofa and sat down in the armchair next to Mateo. "You have to *do* something."

"No one can seriously expect *me* to give Peter's eulogy."

"He was your father."

Mateo bristled. "Barely."

"And he loved you."

"A dying man's declaration of love can hardly be taken seriously."

Simon shook his head. "That's callous and mean and you don't believe that."

"Don't tell me what I don't believe."

"He reached out to you. At the hospital he tried to make amends, didn't he?"

"Dying men are desperate, and desperate men say anything."

Simon made a play for Mateo's hand and seized it tightly. He sat on the edge of the chair, placed his wineglass on the coffee table and held Mateo's hand in both of his. "This is a difficult time, I get that. But don't lose your humanity." They held each other's gaze for a long time, and then Simon leaned over and kissed the centre of Mateo's forehead. "You can talk to me about anything, like you always have."

Mateo smiled thinly. "I know."

There was a distance in Mateo's eyes that pained Simon, made him suspicious. Something in that look made it seem that it was silently understood that Liam's presence *had* altered everything.

Mateo pulled his hand out of Simon's grasp and stood. "Let's go for a walk."

Simon smiled as he watched Mateo chug back his wine. Mateo wanted to be alone with him, and that had to be significant, a sign that they were still connected, that they still mattered to each other. Simon stood and followed Mateo to the front door. They put on their shoes and jackets without saying a word to each other. Simon grabbed his wallet and keys off the occasional table in the hall, opened the door and, together, they left the house.

8

Melinda went rigid. "He's what?"

"He's in love with Mateo," Zane said.

"That's absurd." Melinda reached for her glass. "Utterly absurd."

They were in their bright yellow kitchen and seated at the island bar-counter sharing a bottle of Campari. Zane had waited until Xavier had left the kitchen before filling Melinda in on his visit with Liam.

Zane held his wife's hand. "You shouldn't be surprised. You know how he felt about Mateo before he left. I don't think that Liam's ever let go of those feelings. They've solidified with time."

Melinda lifted her glass to her mouth but withdrew it without taking a sip. "And did you encourage him?"

"No." Zane let go of Melinda's hand. "I told him to back off."

"Really?"

"Really." Zane avoided looking at Melinda. "I know back then I kind of encouraged Liam to —"

"Kind of?" Melinda chuckled as she shook her head. "You had that man high on fairy dust. And when it all backfired —"

"I know." Zane shrugged. "But I was so sure then, about Mateo and Liam."

"That's what you get for trying to play matchmaker." Melinda wrapped her arm around Zane's shoulders. "You're lucky Liam still talked to you after that. I know I would have kicked your skinny white ass from here to kingdom come."

"I like it when you talk dirty to me." Zane winked.

Melinda withdrew her arm from around Zane. "You're incorrigible."

"I know."

"But I don't like this, Liam being here and in love with Mateo."

Zane nodded. "I know."

"I mean, I have a bad feeling about this."

"I know."

"A really, really bad feeling."

9

Mateo and Simon, walking side by side, arrived at the Starbucks on Spring Garden Road where Simon had spent a good part of the day. They went inside and ordered decaf lattes, speaking to the barista without acknowledging each other. Outside, they stepped back into the silence that accompanied them, unsure of how to proceed. They started walking, Mateo leading the way, retracing their earlier steps. Simon was too afraid to break the silence. So he followed along and didn't say a word.

Not far from their house was St. Mary's University, and Mateo diverted them towards the campus. They sat down on a bench near the soccer field, the light from the lamp pole a few feet away shining down on them, and revealing their tired faces etched with the pain of wounds past and present.

Mateo, hunched forward, turned to Simon. "I met Liam before I came out," he said dryly. "About three years in fact before that great moment. Maybe he sensed what I wasn't quite ready to admit at the time. I don't know. I tried to resist him at first, his friendship, I mean. But he seemed to always be around Zane, and any time I was at Melinda and Zane's Liam seemed to just pop in for a visit."

Simon gave a nervous laugh. "You make it sound like the two of you were fated."

"In a way, I think we were," Mateo said, matter-of-fact. "Oh, not like that," he added as Simon twisted his face into knots. "Fated to be friends, if you really believe in that sort of thing. Liam was older, and it was cool to hang out with someone older. Back then, too, I used to run, and he and I started running together."

"You, run?" Simon laughed grandly. "Really?"

"Yes, really." Mateo sucked his teeth. "I stopped running because I twisted my knee and running on it became too painful."

"Did you know Liam was gay when you met him?"

"No." Mateo chuckled. "He was, at the time, engaged to be married."

"Oh."

"Yeah, but that didn't last long." Mateo leaned back and tapped his fingers on the sides of his paper cup. "Maybe it was because of us running together, and seeing him so often at Melinda and Zane's, but Liam ended up becoming a good friend, someone I could confide in. He became like a big brother to me, or that was how I came to think of him."

Simon stretched out his right arm and rubbed Mateo's upper back between his shoulder blades. "Something happened to change that?"

Mateo shrugged. "After I came out, Liam made sure I was okay. We went out for drinks, or dinner, or caught a movie. He took me out on my birthday. He and I organized a surprise party for Melinda and Zane's fifth wedding anniversary. He seemed to still be interested in girls though, or pretended to be. I had no idea…" Mateo felt himself becoming emotional, inhaled and continued. "He was there for me, no questions asked, during a period in my life when I had no one, so to speak. I shouldn't say no one. Melinda and Zane have always been there for me. I didn't feel that I could tell them everything, you know?"

"But what happened between you and Liam to change that?" Simon asked cautiously, unsure if he wanted to know the answer.

"New York," Mateo said. "Liam and Zane were at the top of their class when they graduated law school. Liam was actually number one in the class and Zane was number three. They were both taken on by the top law firm in the city where they had completed their articling." He paused. "It was the week of Melinda and Zane's sixth anniversary that Liam received the job offer in New York City. An amazing opportunity, one that we all knew he couldn't pass up." Mateo tried to discreetly wipe away the tear from the corner of his eye. "Liam asked me to go with him."

Simon's eyes widened. "To New York?"

"Yes, to New York."

Simon withdrew his hand from Mateo's back and gulped the remainder of his cold latte. "Is that when he told you that he was in love with you?"

"Yes."

"And you said…"

"I'm here, aren't I?" Mateo rolled his eyes. "Once the shock had worn off, I told him I couldn't go with him, and that I didn't have those type of feelings for him."

"Was that true, that you didn't have feelings for him?"

"No."

"Oh … *oh*…"

"I had had, at various times, a sort of crush on him. I mean, that was normal given everything that he had done for me." Mateo hunched his shoulders. "Christ, I was twenty-one. What did I know about love?"

"And now?"

"Now everything is tangled up in Peter's death and I don't know what to think." Mateo touched his hand to Simon's thigh and their eyes met, probing for something, anything, to hold them together. "Liam left and never said goodbye to me, never called or wrote. He'd come back to visit but never saw me, never reached out to me. At the hospital, that was the first time I had seen or spoken to him in eight years."

Simon placed his hand on top of Mateo's, hoping to feel some type of connection again. "Now, after all of these years, you've seen him. What do you feel for him?"

"Nothing," Mateo said sharply. "Okay, that's not exactly true. I feel numb, like I don't know what to feel. I'm not in love with him, if that's your concern. But Liam … I guess I'm curious as to why he's back here now, if it's permanent."

"You want to see him," Simon said reluctantly.

"I think I have to." Mateo squeezed Simon's thigh. "I know I've been distant and —"

"You've been absolutely impossible."

Mateo nodded. "You're absolutely right. I've been impossible. I'm sorry about that, but I'm going to be honest with you about my intentions regarding Liam. I'm not going to lie about that or try to see him without you knowing."

"I know I should find comfort in that, but I don't." Simon removed his hand. "It feels like Liam's return has turned everything upside-down."

"I hope you don't include us in that."

Simon flicked his eyebrows and stood. "It's getting late, and I have an early class tomorrow."

Mateo, slow to stand, felt empty inside. Everything *was* turned upside-down because of Liam's sudden reappearance. Mateo had to untangle himself from Liam, from that very different past. That made it necessary, imperative, that he and Liam meet. It was the only way to prevent any more hemorrhaging, to save his life and everything in it that mattered. Seeing Liam was the one, sure-fire way for Mateo to completely close, *une fois pour toutes*, that chapter in his life. *Can I make Simon see that, make him understand?* Walking a few feet behind Simon, Mateo worried that Simon didn't trust him, or his intentions, when it came to Liam. He had to make him see that those cinders of love were extinguished long ago. He had to believe it for himself, too.

They arrived at home, Simon unlocking the door and entering the house first. He kicked off his shoes, dumped his wallet and keys back on the occasional table, and went to head upstairs. Mateo, after locking the deadbolt, moved quickly to intercept Simon, and pinned him up against the front door. They looked intently at each other and Mateo, who had cupped his hands to Simon's shoulders, was now sliding his hands down Simon's chest to his stomach. Mateo slipped his hands around Simon's waist and drew Simon into him. He leaned forward and covered Simon's mouth with his own and there was, for both of them, a certain hesitation, as if it were their very first kiss. It didn't take long for them to find their rhythm, and before they knew it they were upstairs in the bedroom peeling off each other's clothes.

THURSDAY

1

MATEO WOKE UP IN THE MORNING FEELING TRANSFORMED. Maybe it was because of the way he and Simon had made love, at times filled with tenderness, at times rough and savage. They reveled at each touch that made them twitch, held on to each kiss that summoned a from-the-gut groan of pleasure.

They returned to their morning routine of sharing the newspaper and their plans for the day over coffee in the breakfast nook. They shared a passionate kiss at the door, both of them checking the urge to head back to the bedroom, before Simon left for the university. A new day, a new start, and everything before it was a dream, a practical joke gone terribly wrong, or so Mateo wanted to think.

The doorbell sounded. Mateo, seated at his desk proofreading a short story he had been asked to write for a local literary journal, glanced at the clock in the bottom right-hand corner of his computer screen. Ten thirty. He knew exactly who it was. Almost as soon as Simon was out the door, shortly before eight, Mateo's cell phone started vibrating. A text message from Melinda followed by a call. The cycle repeated itself, with Mateo ignoring both the calls and the text messages. But they were enough of a distraction to break his focus, to prove that this was not a new day or a dream. The practical joke gone terribly wrong was in full swing.

"I don't want to hear excuses," Melinda said, barging into the house. She dropped her purse on the occasional table, spun around, and pointed at Mateo the way their mother did when they were young and about to be lectured. "He was your father. Giving his eulogy is a question of respect. Don't interrupt. We need to settle this so we can print the program. The funeral's tomorrow afternoon so it's now or never. You've written under pressure before. You're good at it. It's what you do."

"It's good to see you, too," Mateo said, and moved past Melinda and into the kitchen.

"Well?" Melinda said, exasperated, following behind Mateo. "We don't have to call it a eulogy. Maybe a moment of remembrance."

Mateo set two coffee mugs on the counter. "Coffee?"

"Yes, thank you." Melinda picked up her cup and took a sip. "It would be nice if you, well, participate in some way. For one day why can't we at least act like a family?"

"Because we'd be doing just that. Acting. Everyone would see through the charade." Mateo looked smugly at his sister. "I don't think Simon and I are going to make it."

"Of course you and Simon will attend the funeral. You're giving a speech or whatever you want to call it. Discussion closed. I'm adding your name to the program."

Mateo placed his mug on the counter and shoved his hands in his pockets. "Melinda…"

"Do this for me. Please…" Melinda took a step forward, pulled Mateo's hands out of his pockets and held them. "You need to do this, Matté." Tears crept into her eyes. "I don't know how much more I can take. We have to do something to get this family acting like a family. Oh, Matté, you have to, you just have to do this."

He groaned annoyance at the use of that nickname that always pulled at his heart, and resented how Melinda could, somehow, always seem to manipulate him into doing something he was, by instinct, against. Did he have the power, the courage, to resist? To hold his ground? He applied a little pressure to Melinda's hands. "I can't. Don't ask me again."

Melinda jerked her hands away. "Fine." She wiped the tears off her face and reached for her coffee mug. She went to take a sip of her lukewarm coffee but tears were once again in her eyes and she began to sob uncontrollably.

Mateo took Melinda's mug from her, set it on the counter, and drew her into him. He held her, rocking her gently back and forth until she stopped crying. They pushed apart, Melinda looking down and trying to hide her face. Before Mateo could say anything, Melinda slipped out of the kitchen and into the bathroom at the end of the hall beside Mateo's office. When she returned to the kitchen a short time later, she found Mateo leaning against the counter and looking concerned.

"I'm okay," Melinda said, and picked up her mug. "I always thought death brought families together. In our case, it seems to be that death keeps tearing us apart." She took a couple of sips of her coffee. "But you don't seem to care."

"I'm not taking the bait, Melinda."

"Will you at least come to the funeral?" Silence. "I've always loved you, Matté. I've always been there for you when —"

"Don't, Melinda." Mateo's eyes sidled the clock on the microwave. "You can't guilt me into any of this. And, for Christ's sake, don't call me that."

"I don't know why I even bother."

"Now you sound like Doris." Mateo shoved his hands back in his pockets. "Do you know where Liam's staying?"

"Don't go down that road, Mateo."

"I don't have a choice. I need answers that only Liam can give me."

"What about Simon?"

"I've told Simon about Liam, and the fact that I'm going to see him."

"That'll be a mistake." Melinda took one last sip of her coffee, set the mug down on the counter with a loud clank, and backed out of the kitchen. Making for the front door, she grabbed her purse off the occasional table. "There's a visitation this afternoon at two and another one at seven. What you do with that information is up to you."

Mateo made a mad dash for the front door, throwing himself up against it. "Where's Liam?"

Melinda looked pityingly at Mateo. "I care about you, and Simon, too much to help you throw everything you have away. If you want to talk to Liam, find him yourself." She shoved Mateo aside, opened the door and left the house.

Mateo thrust the door shut and slammed his fist against it. *Calm down. Think!* He strode to his office, sat down at his desk and his fingers darted across his laptop's keyboard. Moments later he was searching the online people finder he sometimes consulted. He found one listing for Susan Robertson in Halifax, picked up the phone and dialled. A male voice answered and Mateo eventually got out, "Liam ...?"

"Yes."

"It's Mateo. We should meet..."

2

"WHO ARE YOU LOOKING FOR?" ZANE ASKED. STANDING behind Melinda, he cupped his hands to her shoulders.

Melinda clasped her hands together and held them to her stomach. "Mateo. I thought he might come. He needs to be here, only he can't see that, or won't see that. I don't know…"

Zane moved in front of Melinda and drew her into him. He kissed the side of her head as he held her. "You know how stubborn Mateo is. It's kind of a family trait."

Melinda shoved Zane away and swiped at him playfully. "Maybe you could talk to him?"

Zane shook his head. "No, thanks. That'll only put me in the middle of him and Liam."

"Well, he won't listen to me, about Dad's funeral or Liam."

"Then let him be." Zane wrapped his arm around Melinda. "It's nice to see so many people come out." It was mid-afternoon, and they were at Memorial Funeral Home for the first visitation. "I still think we should have let Xavier come. He wanted to. It would have better prepared him for the funeral tomorrow."

"This is too macabre. When he gets older he'll see enough of death. Right now I want him to enjoy his youth and innocence."

"Oh, Melinda and Zane," Susan Robertson said as she approached the couple. She was wearing a dark navy suit with a matching wide brim hat and holding a pair of blue satin gloves. "I'm so sorry for your loss." She hugged Melinda and then Zane. "How are you holding up?"

"All right, thanks," Melinda said, teary-eyed. She reached for Susan's hand. "It's so thoughtful of you to come."

"I admired your father very much," Susan said, "and voted for him every time. I had always hoped that he would run for mayor." She squeezed Melinda's hand and let go. "He was a great advocate for the people and a champion of the city."

"Yes, he was," Zane said.

"I wonder if I could have a moment with you," Melinda said to Susan, trying to make it sound like it was optional when in fact it was a summons.

"Well, of course," Susan said.

"Melinda…" Zane recognized the perkiness in her voice and knew what it meant. "Now's not the time."

"Sssh." Melinda waved Zane off as she led Susan towards the exit of the funeral visitation room and into the long corridor. "Liam's back in town … How's he really doing?"

"Oh, I really don't know." Susan looped her arm through Melinda's. "He seems so … conflicted."

They turned down the short hall on the left and stood in front of the door with the sign, "Employees Only."

"How so?" Melinda asked.

"It's just…" Susan pulled her arm away and shrugged. "He's caught up in the past and doesn't know how to move forward. I don't think he even knows what he wants. And of course Mateo —"

"What about Mateo?" Melinda asked, panicked.

"Liam's obsessed with him." Susan sighed. "He says he's in love with him."

"Be that as it may," Melinda said, businesslike, "I won't let him destroy Mateo's life. Simon's good for Mateo. He's been able to peel away Mateo's bitterness. And they're happy together." She'd witnessed first-hand how far Mateo had come, and she wasn't about to let Liam ruin everything. She remembered how broken Mateo was after coming out to their parents. The anger burned in his eyes, numbed the muscles that made a smile. She didn't see him smile for over a year. He threw himself into his studies and writing, which helped him to achieve top grades and succeed as a writer. But he was alone and unwilling to trust anyone. It was like he'd lost faith in humanity. Their parents' reaction frustrated her, embarrassed her even. It was clear that being a gay black man in this family wasn't going to be easy. She never expected the silence and hate to endure. It became a sort of personal mission for her to not let anyone else hurt her baby brother like that again. Especially after Simon Denault came into Mateo's life. It was as if someone had waved a magic wand. For Mateo, Simon's presence had stripped away a season of doubt and fear.

"I've tried to tell him," Susan said.

"He needs to stay away from Mateo." Melinda's tone was firm. "It's the only way, I think, for both of them to not completely destroy themselves."

"Well, yes, I think you're right. But … oh, dear … it may be too late, though."

Melinda reached for Susan's arm. "What do you mean?"

3

Liam walked into Grindstone, a pub on Argyle Street, and immediately felt his heart race. *Stay calm. Stay focused.* Conversations collided in the air. Metallica thumped in the background. Servers jockeyed for the bartender's attention as they shouted their orders. The scent of garlic and fried chicken invaded his nostrils and he gasped. Ten minutes past one, and Liam was early for his meeting with Mateo, which was set for one thirty. The lunch crowd had yet to disperse. Why had Mateo suggested such a busy location? One of the servers led Liam to a table at the back of the pub, near the pool tables, where it seemed quieter. A redheaded server appeared and Liam ordered a beer. He could still feel himself shaking. Mateo's call had sent him into a tizzy, made his head spin, and brought the past and his old feelings back to life. Despite his mother's warning, Liam's expectations were high and he wasn't sure he could hold them in check.

Liam gave a wry smile to the female server who brought him his drink. He sat there, inhaling and exhaling, with his head slightly bowed and his gaze held to his beer. He looked up as a shadow fell over part of the table. He shot up out of his chair, nearly knocking over his beer stein, and extended his hand. "Hey."

"Hi," Mateo said, offering a quick handshake.

They sat down, Liam smiling giddily and unable to look at Mateo for more than a few seconds. On the night of their first grown-up exchange during the Christmas social at Melinda's all those years ago, Mateo had made Liam feel weak and impotent. Liam was overwhelmed by that same feeling now, surprised by how easily it had been exhumed. This was the moment when he wanted to be strong, manly, significant. He took a swig of his beer and lifted his gaze. "I'm glad you called."

"What can I get you to drink, Mr. Borden?" The young redheaded server was back and smiling broadly.

Mateo pointed at Liam's stein. "I'll have the same."

"When I walked in here I couldn't picture it as one of your regular hangouts," Liam said.

"It's not."

"Oh…" Liam could feel the heat rushing into his cheeks. "So you really *are* a celebrity."

"I don't think so." Mateo leaned back, out of the way, as the grinning server set his drink down on the table. "Thanks."

"Are you interested in seeing menus at all?" the server asked, staring intently at Mateo.

"No, thank you," Mateo said. "We're fine at the moment."

"If there's anything you need, Mr. Borden, anything at all, let me know." The server offered a coy smile before walking away.

"Wow. Is it like that everywhere you go?"

"No." Mateo took a swig of his beer. "Thanks for agreeing to meet. I know I was a little harsh on you when we saw each other at the hospital."

"There was a lot going on that day," Liam said.

"And seeing you was a shock," Mateo said, matter-of-fact.

"To be fair…" Liam ran his index finger around the rim of his beer stein. "I didn't tell anyone that I was back, which didn't exactly endear me to Zane or Melinda."

"To be fair…" Mateo weighed that up and curbed his urge to laugh. "How fair was it that I never heard from you for eight years?"

Liam opened his mouth to speak but said nothing. He took in Mateo's harsh look that made him nauseous. "I don't … I don't know what to say."

"Start with why you're here," Mateo said bluntly.

Liam gave a nervous laugh. "Things didn't really work out in New York."

"What things? Be specific."

"Christ, don't bite my head off."

"Believe me, Liam, I'm doing everything in my power not to deck you. And it's the first time in my life that I actually want to hit someone."

Liam, stunned by the statement, flinched, as if he was already trying to duck Mateo's right hook. "I get that you're angry —"

"Do you?" Mateo's eyes widened. "I don't think you have any idea."

"I never meant to hurt you, Mateo."

"But you did."

There was a silence. People swirled about them but somehow they remained separate from the crowd. They didn't make eye contact, as if that helped to lower the tension, calm their anxious minds. Liam was taken aback by Mateo's anger. He may have cut him loose, but it was Mateo who had moved on — fell in love and built a life for himself. Did Mateo's anger prove that maybe, just maybe, he was in love with him?

"Mateo, I —"

"I thought we were friends, best friends," Mateo said, his gaze trained at Liam. "When you asked me to go to New York…" He pursed his lips and bit down on them until it hurt. "I was blindsided, and you expected me to turn my life upside-down with less than a week's notice. I mean, fuck … I was at the beginning of my own journey, and the choice before me was an impossible one."

"It wasn't impossible."

"It wasn't easy." Mateo picked up his drink. "What was I supposed to think of your declaration of love?"

"That it was real and true."

"It came out of the blue."

"Did it?" Liam flicked his eyebrows. "We were pretty close. I think that, eventually, we would have taken it to the sexual level."

"How? You were engaged to Lisbeth."

"I broke off the engagement. Because of you."

"Because of me?"

"Yes." Liam nodded. "Because of you."

"Then why did you wait almost a year to tell me how you felt?"

"Because I, um —"

"Oh, for Christ's sake…" Mateo rolled his eyes. "Spit it out already."

"You started dating that rugby player."

"I told you that was simply a booty call. Don't try to put your own cowardice on him."

Liam drew in a deep breath, held it, and pushed it out through his nose. He blinked rapidly, trying to force back the tears pooling in his eyes. "Why are you being so mean?"

"Mean? You think I'm being mean?" Mateo shook his head. "This is me holding you to account."

"You're being mean." Liam looked down. "But I did love you, and I wanted you to come with me to New York."

"Well, at the time, it shocked." Mateo waited for Liam to look up. "And then you left, and I never heard from you again. Not a bloody word."

"What did you expect?" Liam said, raising his voice and attracting the attention of the group seated a few feet away. "I was in love with you. I couldn't be around someone who didn't love me."

"I did love you," flew out of Mateo's mouth before he could retract it. He sighed. There was a brief silence, after which he added, solemnly, "I just didn't know it then, in *that* moment. But you were gone. Maybe if you had returned my e-mails or calls things could have been different. When you didn't, I knew I had lost you. I'm not saying that I would have moved to New York, but we could have had a real discussion about our feelings then and not eight years too late."

Liam took a huge swig of his beer. It seemed like he was going to chug it until it was gone but didn't. "You want to know why I came back?" he said harshly. "I came back because I hated everything about my life in New York. I hated my job because I let it consume me. I hated only meeting guys who always wanted something from me but never gave anything back. I hated being alone in the city. I came back here because the only man I ever loved, the only man I love, is here." His heart raced, almost to the point where he thought he was going to pass out. His eyes were moist but he didn't want Mateo to see him cry. He rubbed the tears away and looked intently at Mateo. *Perhaps if I had returned his e-mails or answered his calls things would be different. Maybe we'd be together now.* "I know you're with Simon, and I know you love him. Yet I can't change the fact that I *love* you, and that I want to be with you."

"Liam…"

"Had I known that you did in fact love me back then…" He paused to find the right words but only came up with, "I don't know what I'm supposed to say now."

"We can't change the past," Mateo said.

"I know that. It's not the past I want to change. It's the present."

"What does that mean?"

"Nothing."

Mateo grunted. "You know, you can't show up here after eight years and say, 'I love you,' and expect that to mean something."

"It means something to me."

"What could it possibly mean?" Mateo was shaking his head. "You're in love with a twenty-one-year-old who no longer exists. You don't know me or the man I've become."

"I've followed your career's every move. I've read all of your books." Liam's thoughts turned to the scrapbook that was still packed away in a box. It was the one thing he did religiously while in New York, and always on Sunday. In the morning, after having coffee and a strawberry Danish at Sugar Café, he stopped at a sidewalk newsstand. He picked up copies of the *New York Times, Globe and Mail, National Post, Chicago Tribune* and the *Guardian.* When he returned home, he scanned the book sections of each newspaper. He cut out any articles or reviews about Mateo and his works, and methodically glued them in the scrapbook. He knew when Mateo's next book was coming out, where the next stop was on a book tour, and what awards he was nominated for and had won. It was a way of staying connected, of feeling like he was a part of Mateo's life. But it was also torture, an unexpected form of punishment. That was because he wasn't really a part of Mateo's life, not in a real way.

Mateo slammed his hand on the table. "That doesn't mean you *know me.*"

"I know you're not really in love with Simon, not in a profound way."

"Excuse me?"

"If you loved Simon, you wouldn't be sitting across from me now because you know that meeting me puts everything at risk."

Mateo's fingers curled into fists. "How dare you —"

"Does Simon even know you're here?" Liam raised an eyebrow. "Then you know it's true. You're simply afraid to admit —"

"Admit what?"

"That maybe you do love me, that you've always loved me." Liam stared down Mateo. "And that Simon ended up being the consolation prize." The next thing Liam felt was the cool liquid hitting his face and stinging his eyes. When they stopped burning and he could see clearly again, Mateo was gone.

Beer dripped from Liam's hair, ran down his cheeks and fell onto his chest. The redheaded server came out of nowhere with a stack of napkins and pointed towards the washrooms behind the pool tables. Liam sat there, the upper part of his shirt drenched and cool against his skin, and one more time felt weak and impotent. He patted his hair and face dry with the napkins, paid his bill and left the pub. He didn't know where to go. Home now felt like any other place, foreign and uncomfortable.

4

Simon Denault walked into the reception area at Memorial Funeral Home. A thin-faced brunette greeted him and directed him to the parlour at the end of the long corridor. He nodded and made his way down the hallway, the soft chatter and sobbing growing louder as he neared. He entered the room, some people turning towards him while most ignored him. He surveyed the dense crowd and, when he spotted Zane standing off in the far corner of the room, headed in that direction. Zane looked relieved to see him and offered a firm handshake that almost made Simon cry out in pain. Simon tried to smile. "Has Mateo made an appearance?"

"I wish," Zane said. "That would solve everything. But at least you're here. An ally at last."

They laughed.

Before leaving the university, Simon had called Mateo, at home and on his cell, but there was no answer. It was a long shot, but he thought Mateo may have changed his mind and gone to the afternoon visitation.

"Oh, you're killing me," Melinda said as she came up on Simon and Zane. She was with Susan Robertson, their arms looped, and both of them simpered, obviously pleased with themselves. "Simon, dearest Simon." Melinda stepped away from Susan and hugged Simon. "How good of you to come."

"I was hoping Mateo was here," Simon said.

Melinda and Susan looked at each other.

"Mrs. Robertson, this is Simon Denault," Zane said. "Simon is Mateo's partner."

Susan struggled for words, but finally smiled and extended her hand. "So nice to meet you."

"What's going on?" Zane shot a concerned look at Melinda. "The two of you are scheming."

"We are not." Melinda glanced down.

Zane's eyes narrowed. "Oh, Christ, don't tell me …"

Melinda swatted at Zane's arm. "Language!"

"What?" Simon shifted his gaze between Melinda, Zane and Susan. "What? Is it Mateo?"

Melinda took hold of Simon's hand. "Don't be alarmed. Susan said Liam went to meet Mateo earlier. I'm certain it's just to talk. I mean, given their history it was inevitable." She watched the colour drain out of his face and squeezed his hand. "Don't panic. Don't think the worst."

"Yes, Melinda's right," Susan intervened. "There's no need to panic. Liam's running amuck. He doesn't know what he's doing. He's in a fog. I'll talk to him." She touched her hand to Simon's arm, then started to put on her gloves. "Well, I should get going."

Susan and Melinda hugged and exchanged words in a whisper.

Zane held out his arm. "I'll walk you out." He led Susan through the crowd.

Melinda grabbed Simon by the arm. "Listen to me. You heard her. Susan's on our side."

"She can't do anything," Simon said, defeated. "No one can. It's up to Liam and Mateo. If they decide —"

"You have to fight for him!"

"Why now? I never had to fight for him before. He was mine. We were happy." Were they happy? Really happy? Simon resisted Melinda's attempts to hold his hand. "I won't fight for him. I shouldn't have to ward off every man who has a thing for my partner. It's not the type of relationship I want to be in. It's up to him. He can come back to me or not. Either way, that's all I need to know."

"Simon —"

"I appreciate your support, but this isn't the time or place to discuss this. Your family needs you now."

"You're my family," Melinda said once she was able to grab hold of Simon's hand. "Don't you forget that." She let go of his hand as Zane reappeared at her side. She turned to her husband. "Fix it!" She slipped off into the throng.

"She means well," Simon said, sharing the sentiment of Zane's rolled eyes. "There are only two people who can 'fix it,' and, apparently, they're holed up somewhere together."

"Let's not jump to conclusions," Zane said. "I spoke to Liam about his intentions, and he assured me that he has no desire to come between you and Mateo."

"Did you believe him?"

"Yes," Zane said quickly.

Simon gave a thin smile. "You're a horrible liar." He placed his hand briefly on Zane's shoulder and then moved off, instantly swallowed up by the crowd.

CHRIST, LIAM, WHAT HAVE YOU DONE? ZANE SEARCHED THE

sea of mourners for Melinda. Edging his way through the multitude, he stopped occasionally to talk with some of Melinda's relatives who were "friendly" with him, but moved on before they ran out of things to say to each other. He caught up to Melinda back in the visitation room, where she and Benjamin were deep in conversation. He approached cautiously in order to eavesdrop on the conversation.

Melinda, when Zane came into view, grabbed his arm with such force that her longish red-painted nails dug into his arm through the sleeves of his suit jacket and shirt. "We have a problem," she said, gritting her teeth.

"I'll talk to Liam," Zane said begrudgingly.

"Fine. But that's not the problem." She loosened her grip. "Well, yes, it's a problem, but now we have another one."

Zane rubbed his forehead. "Christ, what now?"

"Will you watch your language and remember where you are?" Melinda let go of Zane's arm and folded hers. "It's Mateo."

Zane shoved his hands in his pockets. "I told you, I'm not talking to him."

"Will you shut up and listen." Melinda's eyes were wide and angry. "It's about tomorrow."

"The mayor and a number of councillors, past and present, are going to attend the funeral," Benjamin said.

"So?" Zane asked.

"Most of them think that Mateo is going to speak," Melinda said, distressed.

Zane chuckled. "And who gave them that impression?"

"That's not important," Melinda snapped. "What are we supposed to do?"

"First off," Zane said, "tomorrow is about Peter, not the guests in attendance. Second, at the end of the day, no one's going to give a fuck if Mateo speaks or doesn't speak."

Melinda struck her displeased motherly pose with her left hand on her hip and her right hand pointed at Zane. "I'm not going to warn you again about your language." She could tell that her pose and tone, which made Xavier quiver, had no effect on Zane and her arms dropped to her sides. Then she adjusted her black knee-length dress. "He has to say something."

"Let it alone," Zane said. "If Mateo doesn't want to come, that's his choice."

"It'll look horrible," Benjamin said.

"Who cares how it'll look?" Zane pulled his hands out of his pockets and massaged his temples. "I could use a drink."

"Come on," Melinda said to Zane and grabbed his hand.

"Where are we going now?" Zane asked, annoyance bubbling in his voice.

"To see Mateo," Melinda said, as if it should have been obvious.

"No. Stop meddling and let Mateo grieve in his own way." Zane rarely raised his voice to his wife, and immediately felt remorse as Melinda's eyes widened.

"I'm going to see my brother," Melinda said. "If you don't want to come, fine. Find your own way home." She spun around and made for the exit.

"Melinda…" Zane called out but she continued towards the exit. "Fuck," he mumbled, and ran after her.

5

MATEO WAS IN HIS KITCHEN POURING HIMSELF ANOTHER generous amount of scotch. His fifth drink since he returned home from Grindstone, and its effects were beginning to manifest. He felt light-headed, as if the world was turning while he stood still. That was making him dizzy, and at times he thought he was going to be sick. But none of that deterred his drinking, which was the only way for him to blot out his meeting with Liam. He shifted his gaze to his phone on the counter. He thought about calling Simon but what would he say? He had gone to Liam without a word to the man he supposedly loved. He had broken his promise. What did that mean?

The scene at Grindstone — Liam's new declaration of love and his blustering accusation, him throwing his drink in Liam's face — all of it kept playing over and over again in slow motion in Mateo's mind. It felt like a scene written expressly for one of those daytime soap operas his mother used to watch. *Edge of Nowhere* or *Edge of Light* or *Edge of* something. It was dramatic and, for Mateo, regrettable. He could not believe how he had acted, how incredibly juvenile he had been. He had never let anyone rattle him like that, take away his power.

Worst of all, and this was what scared him the most, was that perhaps there was an ounce, and not much more, of truth in what Liam had said. Mateo did not want to believe that he was in love with Liam. That was ridiculous. Wasn't it? How could he love someone who he hadn't seen or heard from in eight years? It was just as absurd as Liam being in love with him. They did not have a history, not one that created a *real* bond. They were strangers, and now more than ever cut off from each other. Yet something, strangely odd and intense, existed between them, and the tiniest of sparks could ignite it. That terrified Mateo, and that was what he had to avoid.

Mateo guzzled back his drink and slammed his glass down on the granite countertop with such force that the glass cracked. He didn't notice though, not at first, not until he went to refill his glass, which then broke into pieces. "Fuck!" There was a stinging pain in his right middle finger. He moved to the sink to wash out the cut and then held a brown dish cloth to it until the bleeding stopped. When he turned around, Simon was collecting the broken pieces of glass and carrying them to the waste bin.

"Thanks," Mateo said, although it sounded more like a grunt. He opened the cupboard door under the sink, stepping aside to let Simon dispose of the broken glass pieces. "I didn't hear you come in."

Simon, closing the cupboard door, looked cagily at Mateo. He didn't speak as he tore off sheets of paper towel, which he used to sop up the liquid from the counter. He threw out the soaked paper towels and washed his hands. Drying his hands on a dish cloth he had taken from the drawer next to the stove, he said, "I stopped by the funeral home this afternoon. I tried to call you to see if you would go but I didn't get an answer, here at home or on your cell."

"I had an appointment," Mateo said, examining the wound on his finger. It still stung a bit. "And why would you go to the funeral home?"

"Because you wouldn't." Simon folded the dish towel and slung it over the oven door handle. "Who was your meeting with?"

"Liam," Mateo said casually, as if it were an everyday occurrence, like checking his e-mail. "We met for a drink at Grindstone."

"Didn't waste any time." Simon folded his arms. "Are the two of you rekindling your old romance?"

"Don't be like that, Simon. We talked, or tried to. And we never had a romance."

"There were deep feelings that neither of you ever explored," Simon said.

"That was a long time ago," Mateo said. He was disappointed, not because of a love unexplored, but because Simon tried to use that against him.

"So you don't love him now?" Simon was leaning against the counter with his hands in his pockets. "All I'm trying to do, Mateo, is figure out where I stand with you."

"It's almost as if you want me to be in love with him," Mateo said, going on the offensive. "Maybe you have someone lined up —"

"Don't turn this around on me," Simon yelled. "I'm not the one secretly meeting up with someone who —"

Ding, dong, ding, dong.

Mateo and Simon stood there staring angrily at each other, and the doorbell sounded again.

"Do you love him?" Simon asked as Mateo went to leave the kitchen.

Mateo stopped at the doorway, turned partially around and said, "I honestly don't know what I feel for him," and went to open the front door. "Oh, Christ, what now?"

Melinda, with Zane in tow, stepped into the house and said, "We have a crisis."

"What isn't a crisis these days?" Zane said and, at Melinda's cross look, shrugged.

"I told you," Mateo said, gesturing Zane to close the door to keep out the humid air, "I don't want anything to do with Peter's funeral. If that's the 'crisis,' keep me out of it."

"You know how well Dad was known in the city." Melinda spoke loudly, like she was teaching a class of rowdy students and trying to dominate. "All those years on city council … Well, the mayor will be there tomorrow and somehow or other he has this idea that you're going to speak."

Zane chuckled. "I wonder how he got that idea? Ouch!" He glared at Melinda, who had stomped on his foot with the heel of her shoe.

"Not my problem," Mateo said.

"He's too busy running around the city trying to conceal his clandestine love affair," Simon volunteered from the kitchen doorway.

"It's hardly clandestine if *you* know about it," Mateo said in a steely voice.

"Oh, Matté, why did you see Liam?" Melinda's voice was filled with emotion. "He's poison. He'll destroy you."

"Now, Melinda." Zane straightened up and used his audacious lawyer voice that he reserved for his opposing counsel in court. "That's a bit harsh, even for you. I mean, Liam's like family —"

"But he isn't family," Melinda shot back. "Not blood."

Mateo covered his face with his hands and drew in a few deep breaths before uncovering his face. "I'm tired of talking about Liam, and I'm tired of talking about Peter."

"I told you this was a bad idea," Zane said to Melinda.

Melinda pointed at the door. "Then go wait in the car."

"I'm going to have a drink," Simon said. "Zane?"

"Oh, bloody hell, yes." Zane made a beeline for the kitchen.

Melinda took a step towards Mateo. "This is a difficult time for everyone. I know Liam's return added to the mix makes it doubly hard for you. But I shouldn't have to tell you that you only have one father, and only one chance to say goodbye. I'm not asking you to stand up before the world and say he was the greatest dad. He wasn't." She paused. "There has to be something respectful that you can say, in a general way. You're right, Matté, this is far from the perfect family. We've let you down. Maybe this is a chance for you to help build us up."

"You're asking a lot, Melinda." Mateo dropped his gaze. "I can't even think straight at the moment."

Melinda took Mateo's face in her hands. "Matté … what's going on?"

Tears streamed down Mateo's face. "I don't know what I want, who I love," he confessed in a whisper, and rested his head on Melinda's shoulder when she drew him into a clenching embrace.

"I'm going to lose him," Simon said.

"Maybe," Zane said bluntly. "Liam's wreaking havoc everywhere. Melinda and I rarely argue but since Liam's been back … every conversation turns into an argument." Zane reached for the bottle of scotch and refilled their glasses. "My advice? Fight. Fight with all your might. Liam's —"

"Why the hell is everyone telling me to fight?" Simon drained his drink. "Am I really expected to fight for a man who, all of a sudden, isn't sure if he loves me?"

"Mateo loves you," Zane said.

"It doesn't feel like it. Fuck…" Simon leaned back in his chair. "Does our relationship even mean anything to him?"

"It's not Mateo," Zane said. "It's Liam. He's used to getting what he wants, damn the consequences. He's at the centre of everything. He was like that in school. If you show an ounce of weakness, give him the slightest advantage, he'll clobber you. Right now he's chasing a fantasy. He's trying to bring the past back to life. That's what, to use Melinda's saying, makes him poison." He clanked his glass against Simon's. "But I can never tell Melinda she's right. I'll never hear the end of it."

Simon smiled faintly. "I don't have any ammunition, nothing to fight with."

"You have five years of loving Mateo and Mateo loving you. Five years of support and encouragement." Zane's tone sharpened. "You've bought a house together, created a home. Don't let Liam be the big bad wolf and huff and puff and blow your house down. Annihilate him."

Simon was shocked by the fierceness of Zane's suggestion. "I want Mateo to fight for us. I want him to see that *we* are worth fighting for. He has to see that. If not … what's the point?" He ran his hand through his hair. "It's just that ... we can't seem to talk to each other, that we don't know how to talk to each other anymore."

"Find a way. Sit Mateo down and don't let him leave until you talk. If it takes all night, so be it. If he tries to walk away, stop him. Fight. Fight with all your might."

The back screen door squeaked open and Melinda came out on the deck, approaching the table cautiously. She stood behind Zane's chair and, at first, placed her hands on his shoulders. Then she leaned forward and ran her hands down his chest. "I'm sorry for stomping on your foot," she said into his ear, "and for snapping at you."

"You should be," Zane said playfully, and turned to kiss her.

"We should go." Melinda stood up straight. "I tried talking to Mateo but it's like talking to a wall." She threw her hands in the air. "I give up." She levelled her eyes at Zane as he chugged his scotch. "I'm starving and I don't want to be late for the next visitation. And we need to get something to take that alcohol off your breath."

Zane stood, stretched out his hand to Simon and gripped it firmly. "Fight." With the handshake released, Zane and Melinda disappeared into the house.

Simon remained seated long enough to finish his scotch before heading inside. His stomach rumbled. He hadn't eaten much all day, and the news of Mateo and Liam together had, at the time, killed his appetite. Inside, he began to pull items out of the fridge to make sandwiches. When the sandwiches were made, he set the two plates on a wooden tray and, despite his better judgment, poured out two more glasses of scotch, which he also set on the tray. He picked up the tray and went first into the living room, which was empty, and then down the hall to Mateo's office. He found Mateo seated behind his desk and staring abstractly at the ceiling.

Mateo, as Simon was about to set the tray down on his desk, said, "I'm not hungry."

Simon, ignoring the comment, placed a plate and glass in front of Mateo. "We're going to *talk*."

"Not now, Si —"

"Yes, now!" Simon slid the club chair from the corner of the room to the front of Mateo's desk and sat down. "If *you* don't want to talk, fine. Then listen. I have plenty to say…"

6

LLIAM PUSHED OPEN THE DOOR TO HIS MOTHER'S HOUSE. He had, as best as he could, dried himself off with the extra napkins that the server had brought him. He smelled like beer. He not only felt humiliated but deflated. Old questions were surfacing again. *What am I doing with my life? Why did I come back here? Could Mateo ever love me the way I love him?* Liam closed the door. Stumbling and lacking the necessary coordination, he tried to take off his shoes. Like a drunk. When he finally got his shoes off, he lowered himself down onto the staircase and sat there, a blank stare on his face.

"Liam…" There was no response. "Liam!" Susan was shaking Liam by the shoulder. "Liam, are you all right?" She kept shaking him as if it were her grip that was holding him up. "Liam!" she screamed at the top of her lungs.

He looked up into his mother's delving blue eyes and as tears banked in his own, he leaned forward and rested his head against her bosom. Susan enveloped him in her arms and held him as he cried. A few minutes later, Liam pulled back and wiped his face with the back of his hands. He didn't say anything, his focus on the corner of the bottom step of the staircase.

"What's that smell?" Susan asked.

"Beer."

"How did you get beer all over you?" She ran her fingers through Liam's hair. "And in your hair?"

Liam lifted his gaze. "It's what happens when you get beer thrown in your face."

"Who would…" Susan's heart sank. "Oh, Liam…"

"He won't admit that he's still in love with me," Liam said, and groaned his disbelief.

"Are you sure that he ever *really* loved you?" Susan asked, and was not intimidated by Liam's harsh look. "You must see how strange and shocking all of this would be for him. He's living a perfectly happy life and then you show up, wanting to implant yourself in his life again."

"Yes, he loves me. I can see it in his eyes. I think he's just torn. He doesn't want to hurt Simon."

"You expect him to walk away —"

"I expect him to be courageous and follow his heart."

"And what if his heart is with Simon?"

"I don't believe it is."

Susan pulled out the chair to the writing desk that was in the hall and sat down, her hands clasped together and resting on her lap. "My dear, sweet Liam … I'm going to say something that you might find hard to hear, you may not even want to see the truth in it, but you must. *You* are in crisis. You're lost and don't know what to do with your life. Somehow practicing law has lost its allure, and instead of finding a new path for your life, you're meddling in the lives of others, causing chaos and confusion."

"The only thing I'm certain of right now is my love for Mateo."

"Are you deluding yourself?"

"No."

"He may love you, but he may not want to be with you. Can you handle that?" Susan reached for Liam's arm and gripped it. "Aren't you, just like you did back then, asking him to give up everything?"

"I don't see it as him giving up everything as much as him going to where the truth lies."

"That's a matter of perspective." Susan removed her hand. "If you continue down this path you will not only lose Mateo, but also Zane and Melinda. They won't stand by and watch you hurt someone they care so much about."

"So now you're in collusion with them?"

"Liam…" Susan shook her head. "Are you willing to lose everything for a love that, potentially, won't manifest?"

"I've already lost everything." He stood. "I'm going to get cleaned up."

"Don't be so negative," Susan said.

Liam mounted the stairs and headed for the bathroom. He washed his face but the beer smell lingered. He hopped in the shower, eager to wash away the stomach-turning stench that brought with it that metallic taste in his mouth. It was a sort of cleansing, of his disappointments and regrets, and that he hoped would let him recapture the childhood dreams that once carried him.

DOES HE REALLY BELIEVE THAT HE'S IN LOVE WITH MATEO? Susan wondered as she rose and returned the chair to the writing desk. She went into the kitchen to make herself a cup of tea. *He wants Mateo to go to 'where the truth lies,' yet he's unwilling to go there himself.* That assessment became her call to action. She wouldn't let Liam end up like his sister and lose himself in some "unholy" quagmire. She hadn't intervened with Cassandra, a mistake that, all those years ago, haunted her now.

The faint sound of the shower running brought tears to her eyes. She suddenly remembered that day, although she didn't know it then, when Cassandra began to slip away from her. It was a Saturday morning, the rain falling in persistent tepid sheets as she returned home from her UCW meeting. She entered the house, taken unawares by Cassandra's booming laugh, so long absent, that drowned out the other unfamiliar voices. She stood in the living room doorway, her eyes first falling on the copy of the *Watchtower* on the coffee table, then locking on the two women seated on the sofa. Jehovah's Witness. In her home! Almost immediately the women stood and took turns hugging Cassandra before stampeding out of the house.

She didn't know then what to say to Cassandra, who quickly scooped up the literature the women had left behind and took refuge in her bedroom. She wanted her children to be open and respectful of other religions, but there was something, a sort of block, that made her distrust Jehovah's Witnesses without really knowing why.

In the weeks that followed, everything changed. Their mother-daughter talks grew more frequent, and Susan felt their connection deepen as Cassandra talked to her more about her studies in social psychology. Her heart sank as she learned, for the first time, about the bullying incidents during high school and how now all was forgiven. She was a little unsettled as girls she'd never seen in the neighbourhood showed up at the door asking for Cassandra. She noticed the abrupt change in wardrobe, skirts and dresses only, but said nothing. Cassandra, who never had many friends, had "come alive," and Susan was happy for her. Yet she struggled daily to not dissuade Cassandra's interest in that religion even though she feared it would come with a cost.

The cost, coming in the last year of Cassandra's graduate studies, was high.

Susan shouldn't have been surprised, but she was, when Cassandra came home and announced she was becoming a Jehovah's Witness. She hadn't realized how tightly Cassandra had latched onto the religion. Wasn't it just a phase? The shock turned into disbelief when she learned her daughter was engaged to a Jehovah's Witness whom she'd neither known about nor met. Then Cassandra was gone. Several years later, Cassandra never called, never came to say goodbye as her father lay dying. That was when Susan realized that not intervening in the beginning had taken her daughter from her life. Now she had to act with Liam because if she didn't, she feared losing him, too. She couldn't lose him and wouldn't let him, involuntarily or not, abandon the people who mattered to him most.

The whistling kettle made Susan look up at the ceiling. *Oh, Liam,* she thought, *can't you see how badly this will end?* She wiped the tear from her eye and turned off the burner. She reached for her purse on the counter and searched for the piece of paper Melinda had handed her at the funeral home. Then she slipped down the hall into what Liam called his office, picked up the phone and dialled. "Melinda? Oh, so glad that I caught you. I thought you'd like to know … we have a problem!"

7

As Simon spoke, Mateo stared blankly at him but the words bounced off him, could not penetrate the thick armour protecting him. He watched Simon's mouth open and close, his minimal hand gestures, like a scene out of one of those early Bill Patton films. *The Last Chance* or something, one his father used to go on and on about. Was Simon out for justice, too? And Simon, often looking past Mateo, was unrecognizable. Not because Simon had become a stranger but because Mateo had been transformed. Mateo was the stranger, had stepped outside of himself, had suffered some kind of "break."

"I just want to talk," Simon pleaded. "I'm going crazy here, imagining the worst but, most of all, not knowing." He emptied the bottle of scotch between his and Mateo's glasses. "Lately I've thought a lot about the early years of our relationship, and how easy everything was between us. Now … it feels like I don't really know you."

When Simon paused to sip his drink, Mateo said, "Stop."

"You're not even listening to what I'm saying, are you?"

"No." Mateo got up from his chair and moved around to sit on the edge of the desk. He took Simon's hand and held it in both of his. "I'm sorry for all of this. I don't know what's happening. I know I don't have any right to ask this but I'm going to anyway." When Simon looked away, Mateo took his hand and touched it to Simon's chin and lifted his head until their eyes met. "I need you to trust me."

"Trust you?" Simon yanked his hand out of Mateo's grasp. "How can I trust you when you're not telling me anything?"

"I need time to think," Mateo said, exasperated. "I can't do that with everyone coming at me from all directions."

"What does that mean exactly, that you 'need time to think?'" Simon, feeling queasy, briefly covered his mouth with his hand. "Does that mean you need to figure out if you still want to be with me?"

"It means exactly that I need time to think. Not about you or Liam or us. Just *think*. Get everything out of my head. Try to draw a blank."

"That somehow negates us, makes us irrelevant."

"You keep pushing for an end to us."

"That's not true. I want to know if there is an 'us,' or has Liam already succeeded at smashing that?"

"You're not being fair, Simon."

"Neither are you." Simon stood, collected the empty plates and, carefully sipping his scotch, made for the door. He turned halfway into the room and said, "I'm told I should fight for you. The thing is … I know I've already lost you. Maybe not to Liam per se, but I've lost you all the same. I don't know what happened between last night and the time after I left for the university this morning but…" Simon blinked rapidly to dispel the tears mounting in his eyes. "I don't want to wait. I don't want to… Let me make it easy for you so you don't have to choose."

"Simon —"

"Isn't this what you want? I can't compete with Liam Robertson. I don't have his looks, his money, his charisma."

"You're being silly."

"Then tell me, now, that you love me, that you want to be with me."

Mateo dropped his head.

Simon's chest tightened and tears streaked down his face. "Then I guess we're done. If you want to know exactly what that means, it means that I'll be sleeping in the guest room starting tonight." At the door he turned around. Would Mateo tell him not to go, offer some type of conciliatory act? Not a movement, not a sound, so Simon left the room.

Mateo, still seated on the edge of the desk with his head hanging low, went numb. He drew in a long, deep breath and slowly pushed it out through his nose. In a life that had been built through heartache and pain, he had arrived at a moment of triumph when Simon came into his world. Simon had turned the notions of love and family on their head in a way that gave Mateo hope for the future. How quickly that had all slipped away, and Mateo wasn't sure, or if it were necessary, for it to be put back together. Perhaps Liam's return had only revealed the fissures, long concealed, in their relationship that neither of them was ready to face. Mateo stood and left his office, and the house that was no longer home, unsure if it could ever be home again.

FRIDAY

1

THE TALL REDHEAD OGLED SIMON ALMOST FROM THE MOMENT he entered Lair, the latest gay pub to pop up in the city. When Simon walked into the cosy establishment, shortly after midnight, he wasn't surprised to see that every stool at the long bar was occupied with beer-thirsty men. With its unique and somewhat eclectic offering of twenty-two draught beers, Lair was a popular venue where locals gathered to watch *Hockey Night in Canada* on Saturdays. Straight men came for the beer and hockey, at times oblivious to the cross-dresser who, seated next to them, almost succeeded at picking them up. Nor did they seem to mind, not publicly anyway, having strange men buying them drinks. Saturday nights at Lair meant all bets were off. And Lair had become, in the year it had been open, Simon's refuge when Mateo was away. He was friendly with some of the regulars, flirty and coy even, but revealed few personal details about himself.

But this wasn't a Saturday night. It was Friday, twelve thirty-six. In the morning! At the very back of the pub was a small stage with a tall drag queen dressed up as Cher lip-synching "If I Could Turn Back Time," and badly at that. Even the pointing and cackling laughter could not move the Cher impersonator from the stage. Simon dropped his gaze as he walked past the familiar-looking redhead and to the far end of the bar. He ordered a beer, didn't care what kind, paid for it and sat down at the one free table jammed in the corner between the bar and the fireplace. He watched as impersonator after impersonator took to the stage, paying tribute to Madonna, Céline, Bette and others, and wondered what it was like to *be* someone else. Or pretend to be. Was it some form of escape, a way to dull a deep and monstrous pain? Were they truly transformed? Was this their ultimate life-saving force?

Four hours after walking into Lair, Simon knew he needed saving — from the present and the past — from himself. He was in the middle of a meltdown, tied down by a sinister force ravaging his core. He had failed to hold up his promise — to Mateo and to himself — to nurture their love, to be faithful and true. The events of the past few days had injected a fast-moving, degenerative virus into his moral core. He had slipped badly, into darkness, away from his centre, away from everything he believed about love and family and truth.

"You don't have to go," the deep voice said.

"Yes, I do," Simon said, standing in the middle of the dimly lit room. "This shouldn't have happened, Kevin. It was a mistake."

"What?" Kevin scratched the top of his full red mane. "Do you want to pretend instead like we don't know each other?" But they did know each other. Intimately. During the second year of his doctoral studies, Simon had met Kevin Milbrook, and for eight months they carried on a torrid sex affair. The liaison ended because Kevin, a Grade 9 math teacher, moved to Inuvik to teach for a year.

"Just help me find my keys." Simon dropped to his knees and patted the floor with his hands. No keys. "Fuck."

"They're probably in the sofa." Kevin slid off the sofa and started to pull up the cushions. "Don't you remember?"

"Remember what?" Simon said.

"The last time we had sex together."

Simon shook his head. "No." He didn't want to remember the time, three years ago, when Mateo was off on a book tour. Mateo was then, more so than now, the golden boy of the literary scene, and always in demand. Simon felt neglected, like he didn't matter to Mateo. So Simon went out one night to Reflections Cabaret and ran into Kevin, whom he hadn't seen in nine years. Simon drank considerably that night and, involuntarily or not, fell under the spell of the man with whom he had been involved. Desperate to *feel* loved, Simon eagerly accepted Kevin's invitation into his bed. On that night Simon was riddled with guilt and shame and remorse, but mostly guilt.

Kevin turned, looked quizzically at Simon for a moment and then continued his search of the sofa. He spotted the keys wedged in the corner. "Here." He thrust them at Simon, who was slow to stand.

Simon took the keys and shoved them in his pockets. He then made for the front door, stabbing his feet into his shoes.

"So maybe I'll see you in another three years?" Kevin said primly, as Simon went to open the door. "Am I your go-to guy when things suck at home?"

Simon shrugged, opened the door and stepped out into the calm of the night. Walking hurriedly in the direction of his home, he slowed his pace as he neared Bridges Street. He felt sick and disgusted. *What was I thinking? I wasn't thinking. I couldn't think. I should have stayed home, gone to bed.*

I wouldn't have run into Kevin, wouldn't have let lust and insidious desire rule me. But nothing happened. Nothing serious, anyway. Just kissing. He breathed deeply. He didn't want to think about their past, about his deceitfulness.

It was about five in the morning when Simon entered the dark and quiet house. He tiptoed up the stairs and, like he said he would, went into the guest bedroom. It didn't feel right — Mateo across the hall and stretched out in the bed that they had shared, him voluntarily seconded to a room without meaning. He gently closed the door, feeling an ache that had long been absent. He climbed on top of the bed, still wearing his clothes impregnated with the faint smell of Kevin's cologne. Tears were in his eyes. He knew that he had lost everything in his life that mattered. Whose fault was that? Mateo's! His! No, they were both responsible. "Oh, Christ," he moaned. And just like that night three years ago, guilt and shame and remorse tackled him, but mostly guilt.

2

Mateo was alone in the house. He woke up early, shortly after six, but did not leave the master bedroom. He wrote in his journal and read until he heard the front door bang shut. That was around nine o'clock, when Simon had left the house for the university. Now it was eleven, and Mateo had spent the last two hours making notes, although the page, like his mind, was blank, or half blank. Mateo wasn't sure he could go through with it, but he said he would try.

Last night after the fight with Simon, Mateo had gone over to Melinda and Zane's. He needed to feel like he was a part of something, and Melinda always had a way of shoring up his connection to a world that often felt alien to him. He didn't say much about what had happened between him and Simon, or that they were "done," and Melinda didn't press for details. He just needed to be around family, and Melinda and Zane were all he had.

At one point, when Mateo and Zane were alone in the dining room drinking wine, Zane said, "People noticed that you weren't at either visitation."

"They would never have known who I was if Peter hadn't become a politician," Mateo said. "That made his whole life public, put all of us on display."

"Didn't your own success do that, too?" Zane asked, but the question hung in the air. He raised his arms above his head, crossed them and reached up as far as he could. He repeated this five times before taking another sip of his wine. "Melinda could really use your support tomorrow. I'm not asking you to be there for Peter or anyone else. I'm asking you to be there for her. She's worn out."

Mateo finished off his glass of wine, reached for the bottle and poured himself another generous glassful. "It's going to be a circus."

"That's for sure," Zane said. "It's *your* family."

They laughed.

"Ryan must be happy to be giving the eulogy." Mateo glanced over the program that lay open on the dining room table. In his absence decisions had been made and next to *Eulogy* was Ryan's name. Mateo felt relief, then scrunched his eyebrows. He slid the program towards Zane and pointed with his index finger to *Moment of Remembrance*, beside which there was no name. "What's that?"

Zane gulped his wine. "A sort of ... in case ... if you're there and want to say something, like Peter —"

"Oh, for Christ's sake."

Melinda, returning to the dining room, said, "This is my house. Please mind your language." She sat down in the chair at the head of the table, with Mateo on her right and Zane on her left. She looked tired, like she was about to collapse. "I can't wait until all of this is over."

Zane reached for Melinda's hand. "Tomorrow."

"Thank the Good Lord Mama gets everything," Melinda said, relieved. "I couldn't imagine having to deal with any estate matters, and Ryan believing he should get it all." Melinda's gaze shifted to the doorway. "You should be in bed, young man."

Xavier, wearing his blue pyjamas, came into the room and stood next to his father, who wrapped his arm around him. "I can't sleep," he said, yawning and trying to fight his tiredness.

"Well, you need to try," Melinda said unsympathetically as she worked to stifle her laugh. "Tomorrow's going to be a long day." As Xavier rubbed his eyes and leaned his head against his father's shoulder, Melinda was unmoved. "Upstairs, now!"

"Will you tell me a story, Uncle Mateo?" Xavier asked.

"Story?" Melinda waved her index finger nixing that idea. "You think you're clever, young man, don't you? Don't look at your father. You may look and act like him, but you can't fool me. You told me you were too old for bedtime stories, so up to bed you go." When Xavier didn't move, she shifted in her chair to make it seem like she was about to stand. "Now, I'm going to count to three. One." She tapped the table with her knuckles. "Two…"

"Let's go, Xavier," Mateo said, pushed his chair back from the table and stood. "It's going to be the fastest story in the world." He avoided Melinda's harsh look and followed Xavier upstairs to his bedroom. Xavier was already in bed, with the covers pulled up to his shoulders, when Mateo entered the room. Mateo sat down on the edge of the bed. "Once upon a time … the end."

"Hey, that's not fair," Xavier said, and banged his two small fists against the counterpane.

"I'm letting you imagine what came between the beginning and the end," Mateo said, and winked.

"How come you won't come to Grandpa's funeral?" Xavier asked.

"It's complicated."

Xavier propped himself up in the bed. "Are you afraid?"

"No."

"I'm afraid," Xavier said, "to see Grandpa like that. I wouldn't be scared if you were there."

"Oh, you are your mother's child." Mateo sighed. "There's nothing to be afraid of. But if you don't want to see Peter like that, you don't have to. You don't have to look."

"Mama said Grandpa's gone to heaven. Do you think that's true?"

"What do you think?"

"I guess." Xavier shrugged. "But how do you know for sure?"

"You have to believe."

"Do you believe in heaven?"

"Isn't it past your bedtime?" Mateo motioned his nephew to slide down into the bed.

"You can sit with me," Xavier said as Mateo stood.

"What?"

"Tomorrow. You can sit with me."

"Xavier —"

"Please?"

Mateo, when he saw the tears pooling in Xavier's eyes, sat back down and drew his nephew into him. "Grandpa was very sick, you know."

"I know," Xavier said into Mateo's chest.

"And he loved you very much."

Xavier pushed back and rubbed his eyes. "He loved you, too."

Mateo offered a faint smile. "I think it's way past your bedtime."

"What about tomorrow?" Xavier asked as he fell back in his bed.

Mateo stared intently at Xavier for a long time. At the creaking sound in the hall, he said, "I'll see you tomorrow."

"Promise?"

"Promise."

"Cross your heart and hope to die, stick a needle in your eye?"

"Yes, Xavier. Now go to sleep."

Xavier rolled onto his left side, facing into the wall, and Mateo turned out the light and left the room, closing the door behind him. When he saw Melinda leaning against the wall outside of Xavier's room, he shot her a knowing look.

Melinda rushed at Mateo and hugged him. "Thank you," she said into his ear.

Mateo jumped at the sound of a car door banging shut. He clicked on the mouse a couple of times and then paper shot out of the printer. He scanned the document, his mind seemingly blank again. How could he do this? There he was ready to break his promise, to be his own man. The notes on the page were, if anything, incongruent, and did not mention family, love, or forgiveness. How could he talk about family and love and forgiveness, in an authentic way, when his own home was crumbling down around him?

He left his office and went into the kitchen to refill his coffee. He was about to open the fridge door to get the cream when his gaze fell on the photo of him and Simon taken the previous summer. They were all smiles, seated on their back veranda bench with their arms wrapped around each other. It was Mateo's birthday, and Simon had organized a surprise party for him. They were happy, then, weren't they? Mateo thought they were, despite certain indiscretions that he had overlooked. After finally adding the cream to his coffee, Mateo started to unload the dishwasher, sipping his coffee as he worked. He flinched at the opening and closing of the front door.

Simon appeared in the kitchen and said, "Hey."

Mateo didn't look at Simon, didn't say a word, and continued to put the dishes away.

"Zane texted me and said you were going to the funeral after all," Simon said, trying to catch Mateo's eye. "So I thought —"

"I don't want you there." Mateo closed the dishwasher door and looked blankly at Simon. "If we're 'done,' as you said we are, then I don't want you there."

"Mateo —"

"I'm not a fool, Simon." Mateo leaned against the counter and folded his arms. "You claimed to be so worried about me running back to Liam and ditching us when, in fact, you're the one who did the ditching." He flicked his eyebrows. "I know about you and Kevin. I knew about it when it happened three years ago, and I know about it last night. Christ, this city is so fucking small. No one can mind their own business." There was a silence. "Three years ago I let it pass because I was hardly around, and I blamed myself, like I had driven you away. That was my own stupidity but last night ... that was yours."

"I never meant for last night to happen," Simon said. "I drank way too much, and I was just so angry with you, but it won't happen again." He advanced and tried to hold Mateo's hands but could not manage to unfold Mateo's arms. He cupped his hands instead to Mateo's shoulders. "I *do* love you," he said with urgency.

Mateo unfolded his arms and shoved Simon away. "We can talk about the details later, but at the moment I'd like you to leave."

"Leave? What do you mean, leave?"

"I mean, find somewhere else to live," Mateo said, business-like. "Maybe you can crash at Kevin's. Or there are a number of cheap hotels in the city."

"This is my house, too."

"I'll buy you out."

"Mateo..." Tears streamed down Simon's face. "Don't do this."

"I didn't do this," Mateo barked. "You did." He went to leave. At the kitchen doorway, with his back to Simon, he added, "And I'd appreciate it if you weren't here when I get back," and made his way upstairs.

3

Melinda paced the parlour in the basement of Trinity Baptist Church where the family was gathering. It was one thirty, and there was no sign of Mateo. The funeral was set to begin at two and she hoped that Mateo would keep the promise that he had made to Xavier. She kept pushing Zane away each time he tried to comfort her, so he went to check the main sanctuary for signs of Mateo. All she wanted was to have the entire family together on this day, to for once feel a certain sense of normalcy.

"Mom," Xavier said, tugging on Melinda's hand.

"In a moment," Melinda said.

"But it's Uncle Mateo…"

Melinda spun around. There was Mateo standing next to Zane in the corridor outside the parlour. She marched towards them. She couldn't stop herself from crying. She wanted to hug him but, sensing his reluctance, reached for his hand. "So glad you made it." She quickly surveyed the corridor and frowned. "Where's Simon?"

"He couldn't make it," Mateo said, and pulled his hand out of Melinda's tight grasp.

"Couldn't make it?" Melinda glanced at Zane. "Is he ill?"

"Let it alone, Melinda," Mateo said, and went into the parlour. Approaching Xavier, he said, "Are you still afraid?"

Xavier shook his head. "Grandpa just looks like he's sleeping." Xavier looked nervously around the room. "Uncle Mateo…"

Mateo noticed how everyone was staring at him and how they'd look away as soon as their eyes met. He and Xavier joined Melinda and Zane in the hallway.

"My presence is making a spectacle of this already," Mateo said. "I'm not going to stay."

Xavier said, "But you promised," and yanked on the sleeve of Mateo's suit jacket.

Mateo squatted down in front of Xavier. "I know —"

"You said cross your heart and hope to die," Xavier reminded Mateo sternly.

Mateo bit down on his lower lip. "You're right, Xavier." He stood and looked at Melinda. "I'll be upstairs."

Entering from a door at the front, the buzz of chatter and mournful sobbing welcomed Mateo and set him on edge. The church was packed, but the first five rows in the centre bank of pews had been cordoned off and reserved for the grieving family. He turned towards the choir loft and saw his old friend Roy Smythe. A tingling sensation raced over his body as he thought with nostalgia about his and Roy's friendship years ago. *Was everything simpler then? Or was I just naïve?* The music, the sobbing, the knotted faces made the whole scene feel mournful. Mateo never understood why funerals were always so sad. For the believer, wasn't this what they had worked so hard for? To be going home to be with their Lord and Saviour? Spending an eternity in heaven where there was nothing but peace?

As Roy held the last notes of "How Great Thou Art," Mateo sat down at the piano and struck a few keys haphazardly. Roy jerked his head around and smiled faintly. The message was immediately understood. Growing up Mateo had, up until the time he had given up playing in public, garnered a reputation for jazzing up traditional hymns that were considered "untouchable." One of those hymns, which in that moment he remembered to be one of his father's favourites, was "There's Power in the Blood." As Mateo played the jazzy version, Roy was doing his part on the organ. A man and a woman came forward and picked up the six-string and bass guitars parked next to the piano, and quickly found the key. The uplifting music silenced the chatter and crying, and soon the mourners were clapping in time to the beat. Rolling into the chorus, Mateo glimpsed a woman stand on the far right side of the church and she belted out the words. The soft clapping became thunderous. Half of the people stood, singing along as the singer was improvising with Mateo and Roy on the verses. It felt more like an old-time Baptist revival than a funeral.

At the end of the song came acclamations of "Amen!" and "Hallelujah!" and "Praise God!" Mateo was about to get up when Melinda appeared at the piano. "One more!" She winked and raced back through the door through which she came. Mateo started playing, "Down by the Riverside," joined by the guitar players and Roy on the organ, and one more time the congregation was on its feet, clapping and singing as if their lives depended on it. As Mateo struck the final chord, Ryan appeared behind the pulpit in his black robe, his eyes on fire. Those seated stood as the Borden family walked into the church and took their seats. Mateo slipped from the piano bench and down the far aisle. He stood at the back of the church, eager to escape.

4

AN HOUR INTO THE SERVICE, MATEO WAS STILL STANDING AT the back of the sanctuary, leaning up against the wall with his hands shoved in his pockets. He had wanted to leave, to escape the spectacle that he had earlier been a part of, but he couldn't move. There was a force holding him there, chaining his feet to the floor. He listened to the prayers, scripture readings, tributes and the choir singing, but was unmoved. Nothing stirred in him, nothing made him sentimental.

He was aware too, after his performance at the piano, that people were looking at him. Those who knew him, or knew of him, speculated in hushed voices about why he wasn't seated with the rest of the family. He heard one woman say, "They didn't approve of his lifestyle," in a righteous tone. He struggled to block out the other voices, to not let other people's thoughts become his own. The choir finished singing, "In the Sweet By and By," and Mateo's eyes were glued to the front of the church as Melinda ascended to the platform and stood behind the pulpit. She read a passage of scripture, her voice overcome with emotion. When the reading was done she stood there, looking out into the congregation, as if scrutinizing each face. Even from the back of the church Mateo could tell that Melinda's eyes had landed on him.

"At this time I'd like to call on…" Melinda's voice trailed off. She cleared her throat and then seemed to stare abstractly ahead.

Mateo didn't move, glued to the wall, and no matter where he looked he felt like he couldn't circumvent Melinda's eyes. The silence was broken by a soft chatter that made Mateo's heart race. He watched as heads swung from side to side, waiting to see what would happen next. The voices grew louder, and on the platform Ryan and Melinda stood huddled, deep in conversation. Something happened. Mateo couldn't say what it was, but he was surprised to find himself making his way to the front of the church. The noise fell away in a wave. He could almost hear his heart thumping in his chest.

Melinda left the platform and met Mateo at the bottom of the stairs. She took his hands in hers, tears running down her face, and offered an encouraging smile. She applied a little pressure, let go of his hands, and returned to her seat.

Mateo, his gaze held to the violet carpet, mounted the stairs. Once he was in front of the pulpit, he pulled out the folded piece of paper from the inside pocket of his suit jacket and fidgeted with it. Another soft chatter was on the rise until he lifted his head. "It had been some time since I had spoken to Peter. When he asked to see me at the hospital I thought that it was some kind of bad joke. I was prepared to let the misunderstandings that had, for so long, separated us be taken to the grave. Peter wasn't." Mateo looked down and shoved his hands in his pockets. He wasn't sure he could do this, wasn't sure he had anything meaningful to convey.

"Go on," the familiar voice encouraged.

Mateo laughed nervously and looked up. "That was my sister, Melinda, who has been, or who has tried to be, the bridge. And during the past few days she has reminded me, in a nagging older sisterly way, that despite the past, I only have, er, had, one father." He saw Melinda, sandwiched between Zane and Xavier in the second pew of the centre section, and nodded. "I want you to know, Melinda, that that message has been received loud and clear.

"And despite a certain resistance, despite a certain close-mindedness, all on my part..." He paused. This didn't feel right. What he was about to say didn't feel right. "It wouldn't do any good for me to stand here and rehash the details of my relationship with Peter. I believe I've sufficiently alluded to the fact that it wasn't the best father and son relationship." He cleared his throat. "What I think I'll remember most about Peter stems from our last meeting in the hospital. I learned I didn't really know him. I had made assumptions, I had clung to outdated beliefs about him.

"What I hope you can take away from this is, as Peter reminded me, that when you hold on too tightly to misunderstandings, you risk losing those who matter most to you. You risk cutting yourself off from love. Look around you today and see, really see, those who have lifted you up when you felt like everything was falling down. See those who cheered you on when you took on a monumental project that most thought you were bound to fail at. See those who have accepted you for who you are and not for who they wish you to be and know..." There was an unexpected charge in Mateo's voice. "Know that they are your family because they are there for you no matter what, no matter when."

"Amen," a voice squeaked.

"Life should be about love and understanding," Mateo continued. "Peter reaching out to me at the very end of his journey was about something that he had done for so many years for this city. He was building a bridge. He was trying to bring together two very different and divergent poles. It was his moment of truth, reminding me, reminding you, that there is nothing more important in this life than love. And that love really does have the power to heal, to bring us through any tribulation.

"One of the last things Peter said to me was that he hoped there was forgiveness in my heart, that I could forgive him. It wasn't until recently that I realized that it wasn't about forgiving my father. It was about me being able to forgive myself." He surveyed the crowd. "You've all come here today to pay tribute to a man who worked tirelessly for this city. The best tribute we could perhaps pay to him is this… Where there is strife in our lives, in our relationships, in our communities, try to be the bridge." Mateo took the folded paper and slipped it into the inside pocket of his suit jacket as he left the platform. With his head down, he walked hurriedly down the centre aisle and into the vestibule, collapsing onto a wooden bench where he tried to catch his breath.

5

After the church had cleared out and everyone was on their way to the cemetery, Mateo returned to the sanctuary and sat down in the last pew on the far left side. He wasn't concerned about how it looked, him not going to the gravesite after his speech. His mother sat with her eyes closed the whole time he was on the platform, as if he were too "ugly" to look at, still too much of a disappointment. He constantly dodged Ryan's glares of contempt, which made it hard for him to keep his own anger under control. Now, alone in the church, he was too wound up, teetering between sanity and a breakdown, and feeling for the first time, when it came to his father, a sense of loss.

He couldn't say how long he had been sitting there, somewhat hunched down, staring at the large wooden cross on the wall behind the choir loft and unmoved by it. When had he lost his faith? When had God become a monster instead of a saving force? In a place where so many sought comfort, Mateo was unable to grab onto a presence, to feel something inside of him. He closed his eyes, not with the intention of offering up a supplication, but to remove himself from this place, to escape to another order of reality. Then, at the squeaking sound of the pew as someone sat down, he opened his eyes and looked to the left, and let his head roll backwards.

"I don't mean to intrude —"

"What do you want, Liam?" Mateo said.

"I wanted to see how you're doing."

Mateo looked up at the high ceiling, blinking magnificently, and breathed deeply. "I'm fine. Now please go away."

"Mateo, I'm sorry —"

"It's too late to be sorry." Mateo lowered his head and turned to Liam. "You've wrecked everything."

"That's not fair, Matté."

"Don't call me that."

Liam shifted his body sideways and stared intently at Mateo, who was no longer looking at him. "I love —"

"Stop it!" Mateo was clenching and unclenching his right hand. "You can't love me. You don't know me." Tears flooded Mateo's eyes and rolled down his cheeks. He was in shock at how deep the sense of loss had become, and how he had unknowingly become wrapped up in it. His father was dead, and he now regretted the way he had left things between them. He could hear clearly, "I love you, son," which were his father's last words to him, and he had said nothing in return. *I was so callous*. It was easy for Mateo to believe that he was better than them, his family, for not being caught up in religion yet he was just like them. He had let another kind of hate infest his heart and that made any type of reconciliation impossible. Now the loss of Simon, of a love he wanted so desperately to endure, was present and real, and fused with the grief he felt for his father. But staying in that quagmire would cost him too much, upend him, tear apart his fabric.

"Oh, Matté…" Liam slid his body closer and wrapped his arm around Mateo's body.

Mateo was surprised when his head found Liam's shoulder, and how comforted he was by the act of Liam holding him. He knew it wasn't right, that one more time his power had been taken away. But in that moment it, temporarily, took away his pain.

Melinda passed through the vestibule and found Simon standing near the main doors to the sanctuary. They hugged. After they separated, she followed Simon's distracted gaze into the church. Her mouth dropped open when she saw Liam and Mateo huddled together. She walked light-footed in their direction, hoping not to be detected until the last possible moment. She twitched when Liam kissed Mateo's head. She placed her hand on Mateo's shoulder, and he sat upright.

"Look, Melinda…" Liam stood. "It's not…" He shook his head at Melinda's wild-eyed look, then touched his hand to Mateo's other shoulder. "If you need anything …" He withdrew his hand, shot Melinda a knowing look and slinked away.

Melinda squeezed past Mateo and sat down on the warm pew where Liam had sat. She held his hand. "I'm proud of you."

"Why?" Mateo ran his hand over his face. "I made a fool of myself."

"Is that what you think?" Melinda applied pressure to Mateo's hand. "You inspired me. You inspired us all. And the way you played the piano… Dad always loved how you made the ivories sing." There was a silence. "It's a hard day. You don't have to be alone. Simon's here —"

"I don't want to see him." Mateo looked at Melinda and shook his head at her questioning gaze. "It has nothing to do with Liam."

"Really?" Melinda said, indignant. "The way the two of you were cuddled up here —"

"Simon cheated on me." Mateo looked down. "I asked him to move out."

"Mateo…"

"It's not the first time but…" Mateo scratched his forehead just above his right eyebrow. "I don't think that I can forgive this time. I don't think I want to." He pulled his hand out of Melinda's clutch. "And just because Simon and I are done doesn't mean I'm running straight to Liam. That would be hell."

"Oh!" Melinda sat back in the pew. "I'm sorry —"

"Don't be sorry. You were right after all."

"About what?"

"You said Liam would destroy me. But it wasn't only Liam. I destroyed myself by never telling Simon about Liam. It was a house of cards waiting to fall."

"Come into the hall," Melinda said, "and get something to eat."

Mateo stood. "I'm going home."

Melinda stood and drew her brother into a clenching embrace. They pushed apart and she said, "What can I do?"

"You don't have to do anything. I'll be fine."

They made their way, arm in arm, out of the sanctuary and into the vestibule. They hugged again, and Melinda watched as Mateo left the church. *He looks broken*. She felt a deep, local pain. She knew that he was the strongest of them all and he would find a way to keep going. He had to. If not, the only thing for the rest of them to do was to abandon all hope and to let despair have dominion in their lives.

6

"He had me fooled," Zane said as he undid his tie. "I really like Simon, and I thought that he and Mateo would be together a lifetime."

"So did I," Melinda said with disappointment. "I still can't believe that —"

"You can't worry about that." Zane tossed his tie onto the counter and hugged Melinda from behind, lifting her up slightly like a kettlebell. "Mateo can look after himself. He's proven that."

"I know." Melinda stepped away and grabbed the open bottle of red wine that was on the counter. She filled two glasses and took a sip. "I hope he meant what he said, about not running to Liam."

The doorbell sounded, and they heard the patter of feet rushing down the staircase. By the time Zane made it into the foyer, Xavier had opened the door wide but didn't say a word.

"Hi, Xavier." Liam held out his hand.

"Hi." Xavier looked at his father after the handshake. "I thought it might be Eric. Mom said he could come over and play."

"You don't answer the door on your own," Zane said.

Xavier, understanding his father's stern look, bounced back up the stairs.

"Don't just stand there," Zane said, unable to tamp down the ire in his voice.

Liam came into the house and closed the door. He followed Zane into the kitchen where he was greeted by Melinda's cold, hard glare. "Sis, I —"

"Don't, Liam," Melinda said, curt.

"But what you saw at the church … it wasn't what you think." Liam sounded desperate. "Mateo was upset and I was only trying to comfort him."

"You've been determined to get your way," Melinda said in a steely voice. "You don't care about who else gets hurt."

"You know that's not true," Liam said.

Zane poured out a glass of wine and handed it to Liam. "Let's all try to remain calm."

"You must be happy now that Simon and Mateo are breaking up," Melinda said before she could censor herself.

Liam nearly choked on his wine. "I had no idea." After the shock had settled over him, there was a great pang of joy. He tried not to smile but he was deliriously happy at the news. "But it's not my fault."

"You should have stayed away," Melinda said.

"Melinda!" Zane said.

"Your return has brought nothing but misery," Melinda went on. "You decided to uproot everyone else's lives along with your own, and that's not fair."

Zane, torn between his loyalty to his wife, whom he loved, and Liam, whose friendship he cherished, stomped his foot. "That's enough!"

Melinda threw her hand in the air and glared at Zane. "Well, he's your friend, so deal with him." She stormed out of the room.

"It's not an easy day for her," Zane said.

"Don't make excuses for me," Melinda hollered from the dining room.

Zane rolled his eyes and led Liam out of the kitchen and down the hall to the den. He and Liam sat down on opposite ends of the black leather sofa, and let the silence hang in the air between them. Zane didn't know what he was supposed to say. He tried to understand Liam's position, why he had come back and why he was so eager to be with Mateo. But Zane was, secretly, mostly on Melinda's side. Liam was too intelligent not to be able to see the consequences of his actions.

"Do you blame me, too?" Liam said in a whisper.

"You've got to understand Melinda's position. She's looking out for her baby brother, and she doesn't want to see him get hurt any more than he already has."

"I didn't break up Simon and Mateo."

"Perhaps not directly," Zane said, "but you had to suspect what coming back here would do to him, especially given your intentions."

"I thought I could hold my feelings in check. When I saw him for the first time … everything old was new again, my feelings I mean. They took control."

"You let them take control." Zane sipped his wine. "Liam, do you ever stop and think about someone other than yourself?" He could see that Liam was unsettled by the remark, as if it wasn't true. But Zane never bought into Liam's childish "I'm being true to myself" claim.

"I'm following my heart." Liam tasted his wine. "But now I don't know what to do. I mean, today at the church he let me hold him, and I could feel this fire burning inside of me."

"You need to give Mateo space," Zane said, like a teacher scolding a student for talking back. "You need to *think* about him."

"You don't understand…" Liam said, and drained his wineglass. "He's all I think about."

7

Mateo was back at the house. He changed into a pair of jeans and a blue V-neck T-shirt, and made his way to the kitchen. He was about to pour himself a glass of scotch but stopped when he heard the front door close. He could feel himself trembling and studied the label on the scotch bottle. When he looked up, Simon was standing in the kitchen doorway.

"I came back to change and pick up my things," Simon said. "My suitcases are packed upstairs."

"Good."

"I made a reservation at the Express Inn, and left the number on your desk." A silence. "Maybe I can pick up my mail once a week?"

Mateo shrugged. "We'll figure something out."

Simon, looking intently at Mateo, went to speak but decided against it. Was there any way to prove that his love for Mateo was real? He waited a moment longer, then went upstairs to the guest bedroom, changed and appeared a short time later in the front hall with his suitcases.

"Simon," Mateo said after Simon had opened the front door. "Your keys…"

"This isn't fair."

"Your keys."

"Right…" Simon drawled. He pulled his keys from his pocket and slid the square-topped one off the key ring and set it down on the occasional table. He fixed his gaze on Mateo. "There may not be anything that I can say to you right now to change your mind but…" He put his left hand to his intelligent mouth, pulled it away and said, "I loved you. I *still* love you. I don't know why —"

"Simon, please…" Mateo cupped his hands to the back of his head and then let them drop to his sides. "Just go, please."

Simon, rolling his tightly pursed lips, picked up his suitcases, looked at Mateo one last time, and left the house.

Mateo crossed the foyer and closed the door. He turned over the deadbolt and returned to the kitchen. He thought he would feel some sort of relief but he felt nothing. He could not say for certain if this was a beginning or an end, or if he had ended up somewhere in the middle. Wherever he was, he was searching for a way out.

He stared abstractly into the room, a wave of panic rolling over him. Already he felt that he was in a very different house. Not simply quiet and strange but abandoned. The abandonment of love with its sure path, of a home with its sordid history — the distillation of hope and love from the promise of happiness. That was ridiculous. Happiness could not be promised. It had to be created and nurtured but Mateo had, voluntarily or not, let it go to seed.

He moved into the living room and froze. His gaze locked onto the soapstone carving of a cat that Simon had given him for his birthday the year they moved in together. Mateo had wanted to adopt a cat but Simon was deathly allergic. In that moment something shifted, came into focus, and Mateo had an urgent need to eradicate Simon from the house. He sailed from room to room collecting anything that reminded him of Simon. Photos. Knickknacks. Paintings. Candles. Vases. Magazines that Simon had subscriptions to, like *Hello! Canada*, *Walrus* and *Time*. He went into Simon's office, which was across the hall from his, intent on dismantling it but instead simply walked out and closed the door. The dining room table and the space around it was cluttered with all the items that reminded Mateo of Simon and their life together. He now just had to get all of the stuff out of the house. Then Simon would be, for all intents and purposes, banished from his life, exorcised.

SATURDAY

1

"I never knew Mateo could play the piano," Susan said. "You never mentioned that about him."

"I didn't know," Liam said in a rueful voice.

"Oh…" Susan, peeling apples for a pie, looked at Liam, who was leaning up against the kitchen doorframe. "Well, it was certainly magical, how it transformed the congregation."

"I mean I knew he could play, I just forgot." Liam came fully into the kitchen and sat down at the island bar-counter. "I should never have come back here."

Susan set the peeler on the counter and wiped her hands on her apron. "You came back here with not-so-pure intentions. Don't look surprised. You knew that Mateo was taken yet you still came back here for him. I still don't understand why, after eight years, you suddenly had to make your move."

"I couldn't give myself over completely to another guy because Mateo was always in my head."

"But that wasn't Mateo's fault," Susan said, matter-of-fact.

"How was I supposed to —"

"Let go of the past, Liam. Make your life here, in the present." Susan picked up a large knife from the counter and began to slice the peeled apples. "Your mistake wasn't coming back here. Your mistake is living in the past, wishing to change things that cannot be changed."

Liam looked at his mother. "Mateo and Simon have separated."

The knife slipped from Susan's hand and she fixed her gaze on Liam. "Who told you that?"

"Melinda. I don't think she meant to, though." Liam stole a slice of apple and popped it into his mouth.

Susan, her face plagued with disappointment, shrugged.

"Wait a minute. I didn't break them up, right?"

Susan picked up the knife again. "Perhaps not directly. But can't you see how your presence and not-so-private feelings for Mateo may have had an impact?"

There was a silence.

"What should I do?" Liam asked with an air of defeat.

"Admit your true intentions and then figure out a way forward." Susan tried to offer an encouraging smile but couldn't. That would embolden Liam, and in her heart she knew he couldn't really love Mateo. "You haven't done anything since being back. You're not moving forward. It's like you're stuck in neutral. If you're determined to see this through, damn the consequences, then the only way for you to get unstuck is to make a decision regarding Mateo. Either you make a play for him and go after him wholeheartedly, or you abandon it all once and for all."

"Aren't you against that? Me going after Mateo?"

Susan gathered the apple slices and arranged them on top of the crust in the pie plate. "Do you really want to know what I think you should do?"

"Yes."

"Give Mateo some space. He's lost his father and his partner. His whole life is upside-down. The last thing he needs —"

"I feel like it's now or never."

"Do you think Mateo would see it like that?"

Liam, his eyes becoming moist, stood and went to leave the kitchen.

"Liam…" Susan waited until Liam, at the kitchen doorway, turned to look at her. "Love Mateo if you must, cherish him. But maybe your greatest act could be to love him from afar."

"I don't think I can do that." Liam left the room.

Susan, slicing into another apple, said, "This isn't going to end well."

2

It was the middle of the afternoon, and Simon Denault, walking aimlessly around the city, stepped into Titles to escape the rain. He had let his class go early because he couldn't think, couldn't articulate his thoughts clearly. His life was such a mess. He didn't know what to do, if he could find a fix or if he even deserved a fix. The display near the street front windows caught his attention, and he went over and scooped up the book with the sticker "#1 Bestseller." It was Mateo's latest book, *Beyond Salvage*, which he flipped open. A photo of Mateo stared back at him. He smirked. Mateo's serious, off-in-the-distance look on the dust jacket excited him. *Christ, what have I done? I should have been stronger.* A week ago there was no reason for him to doubt that he and Mateo would be together a lifetime. Now he was trying to imagine a life without Mateo, or the idea that Mateo would run straight to Liam. That made Simon nauseous.

He returned the book to its spot and left the bookstore. Raindrops fell intermittently into his hair, which he was constantly running his hand through. Everything around him was foreign, silent, like he had blocked out the world. He heard the voice calling out to him but ignored it. The voice, too, seemed foreign and unconnected to him. Then he flinched violently at the touch of the soft, warm hand against his bare arm. "Oh, Melinda, hello…"

"I'd like to speak to you," Melinda said, somewhat brusquely.

Simon, with his head hanging low, followed Melinda like he was being dragged to the principal's office. They walked as far as Dresden Row, turned the corner and went a few feet where it was quieter and free of the busy pedestrian traffic on Spring Garden Road. There was a mixture of anger and disappointment radiating in Melinda's eyes, and Simon decided to speak first. He said, "How is he?"

"How do you think he is?"

"It was stupid of me, I know." Simon slipped his hands into his pockets. "I want to blame Liam but I know I can't."

"No, you can't." There was no emotion in Melinda's voice, as if, on Mateo's behalf, she had found a way to cut Simon off. "You only have yourself to blame. And while I support Mateo's decision to throw you out, I do believe, despite your gross ineptitude, that you love him. You loving Mateo is better than Liam loving him. There are things Mateo doesn't know about Liam, things that could change the balance of power." She seemed caught off guard by the sudden wave of emotion, yet emboldened by it. "I need you as an ally."

"Of course." Relief injected a burst of satisfaction like a line of cocaine. That was a dark and long passed period of Simon's life that he had managed to bury. "But how? I mean…" The relief transformed into an inalienable *mal du siècle*, and made him feel like he was about to implode. "I can't imagine Mateo wanting to talk to me. And as for any type of reconciliation…"

Melinda gripped her hands to Simon's wrists, tugging on them until his hands were out of his pockets and clutched in hers. "First, you have to have faith." She spoke with the same reverence that Ryan reserved for his Sunday morning sermons but which had evaded him as he gave their father's eulogy. "Faith to believe in love's power to move, to stir, to compel a change of heart. Second, you need to be determined to win Mateo back, to not give up. It's not going to be easy but I believe it's possible once Mateo has seen Liam for who and what he really is."

"And that would be?"

Melinda laughed. "He's a fraud."

Simon realized that Melinda was laughing at him and his innocence, or more precisely his naïveté. "What do you want me to do?"

"Come to dinner tonight." Melinda released Simon's hands. "We must begin in earnest."

"All right." There was reluctance in Simon's voice.

"Five thirty, then." Melinda, adjusting the strap of her purse on her shoulder, added, "Don't be late," and moved off towards Spring Garden Road.

Simon was shaking. When he thought about any sort of future with Mateo there was only darkness. Now there was a flicker of light but the darkness still overshadowed it. That light, no matter how small it was now, held his hope. And that hope was this: "He's a fraud." Melinda was waging a war, and she had enlisted Simon, who was quite eager to wipe out this particular enemy. Simon checked the time. Seventeen minutes to four. He had just enough time for a trip to the liquor store to pick up a bottle of wine, and then return to the Express Inn he had been banished to for a quick shower before heading over to Melinda's. His body was rocked with angst, not really knowing what version of the future — a life with Mateo or one without him — now awaited him.

3

Simon rang the doorbell at exactly five thirty. The late-afternoon sun scorched, and the twenty-minute walk to Melinda's Ridgewood Drive home left him feeling haggard and grimy. He felt like the world was aware of his treasonous acts, Melinda and Zane anyway, and that he had to impress them, woo them back to his side. Mostly he believed he had to impress Zane who, over the years, he came to see as Mateo's protector. Simon knew, too, that in any type of physical altercation there was no contest. Zane could whip his ass. And didn't Simon deserve some form of ass-whipping for what he had done to Mateo? That was why he had spent too much time fretting over what wine to buy. The liquor store clerk, grumbling at Simon's indecision, smiled when he selected the 2009 Majella cabernet sauvignon. Simon, glancing at the label on the wine bottle, hoped that Zane would be pleased. He heard voices on the other side of the door and ran his free hand across his moist forehead. He could feel himself trembling and looked down, and winced when he saw the large wet spot on his shirt in the middle of his chest. Rushing from the liquor store back to his hotel, Simon was still sweaty after towelling himself dry when he got out of the shower. Now his shirt clung to both his back between his shoulder blades and the front of his chest. "Pathetic," he mumbled as the wooden door flew open.

Zane, in his workout clothes and covered in sweat, towered in the doorway. He stood with his feet slightly wider than his shoulder width apart, ready to bend his knees. "What the fuck —"

"Zane!" Melinda appeared, elbowing Zane out of the way and preventing him from assuming the Square Stance, as if he were in a wrestling match and about to take down his opponent. She held out a hand to Simon. "Do come in," she said when Simon took hold of her hand. She pulled Simon into the house and glared at Zane. "That's no way to talk to *our* guest."

"I don't understand what he's doing here." Zane closed the door and, staring down Simon, cracked his knuckles. "After what —"

"I invited him," Melinda said.

"Why the hell would you do that?" Zane shook his head. "And don't warn me about my language. Christ, it's my house, too."

"Maybe this is a mistake," Simon said, and jerked his hand out of Melinda's loosening grasp.

"No, stay." Melinda's tone softened. She brought her hands to her lips, in prayer fashion, and said to Zane, "I *know* he loves Mateo, despite his infidelity."

"Infidelities," Zane said, breaking the word down by its syllables.

"All right. Infidelities." Melinda loosely clasped her hands together and rested them on her abdomen. "But he's the key —"

"Key to what?" Zane asked, the rage in his voice still trembling. Then Melinda flashed him *her* look, the one where her whole face seemed to relax and her eyes rolled back into her head. The look asked, *Are you that stupid?* "Oh, Melinda, for the love of God, stop meddling." He stomped off towards the kitchen.

Melinda reached again for Simon's hand and led him into the kitchen after Zane. "I'm 'meddling' because you're too blinded by what you call loyalty to see Liam for the fraud that he is."

"I think that's the worst thing that you've ever said about Liam!" Zane's eyes narrowed. "I'm trying not to take sides, to get caught up in the middle of it."

"I think I will go," Simon said and thrust the wine bottle at Melinda before turning to leave.

Melinda pointed her left hand at Simon. "Don't move." She turned to Zane. "Mateo has a right to know ..."

Zane tied his face up in knots. "Know what?"

Melinda shook her head. "About the child."

"Child?" Simon squeaked.

"What child?" Zane said, exasperated, and folded his arms.

"Liam's child," Melinda said, her eyes widening as she watched the colour drain out of Simon and Zane's faces.

Zane levelled his eyes at Melinda. "How long have you known?" Silence. "Jesus! Why would you keep something like that from me?"

"I thought you knew." Melinda was on the defensive. "Liam told me that he told you."

"Well, he didn't." Zane unfolded his arms and drew in a deep breath. "Fuck, I need some air." He moved past Simon, ignored Melinda's outstretched hand, and left the house through the back door.

"Is that the secret weapon?" Simon asked. "That's what makes Liam a fraud?"

"Absolutely," Melinda said.

"And Mateo doesn't know?"

"Not yet."

"But you're planning to tell him?" There was a deep, sick feeling that made Simon's stomach flip. "I *do* love your brother, Melinda. I'd love to get him back but that'll devastate him."

"Temporarily, yes." Melinda, unapologetic, glanced at the label on the wine bottle. "Lovely." The doorbell ricocheted off the listless walls and she handed the bottle back to Simon. "Be a dear and pour us all a drink. We'll need four glasses." At the kitchen doorway, she turned back. "Or would you rather see Mateo run straight into Liam's arms?"

"I'd rather see him happy," was Simon's unexpected response.

"I DON'T LIKE THAT SMUG, TRIUMPHANT LOOK ON YOUR FACE," Mateo said as he entered the house.

"Oh, Matté," Melinda said, grinning, and closed the door.

"And I don't like it when you call me that." He heard the pop of a wine cork and looked towards the kitchen. "It makes me suspicious, especially given who's back in town."

"Don't get me started on Liam. He's far from my favourite person at the moment." Melinda looped her arm through Mateo's and guided him towards the kitchen. "I don't want you to be upset…"

Mateo sucked his teeth. "I knew you were up to something."

Melinda rolled her eyes at Mateo's hard glare and then shoved him into the kitchen ahead of her. "Have a drink. Then try doing something completely foreign, like talking to each other." She picked up one of the glasses of wine that Simon had poured and placed it in Mateo's hand. "Talk to *him*." She collected two more wineglasses and went to join Zane on the back veranda.

There was a long, long, long silence. Mateo, without even taking a sip of his wine, could feel himself slipping into a steep drunkenness. The bright kitchen began to spin. He had spent the day before expunging Simon from the house, his life, and the last thing he expected was to see Simon in Melinda's home. Wasn't she on his side? Now Mateo felt like she was questioning his decision, and that riled him, set him on edge when he felt, finally, like he was calming down, like an addict coming off a high.

"I didn't know you'd be here," Simon said in an attempt to break the harrowing silence. "I wouldn't have come had I known. Not that I don't want to see you but I know —"

Mateo retraced his steps back to the foyer and retreated into the living room. He stood in the middle of the room, sipping his wine and feeling dizzy. *When is it all going to end?* He was tired, beaten down to nothing. He couldn't do this anymore, couldn't let the uncertainty linger. Simon entered the room from the front hall and Mateo, his muscles tightening, looked down.

"Do you remember that —"

"I'm not interested in travelling down memory lane with you, Simon." Mateo sat down on the Victorian-era settee.

Just leave. If he means nothing to me then I should be able to leave. He looked up and said, "I've packed up most of your things. Then I realized that I don't want the house. Maybe you do? If not, I'd like to call Dan and get it listed."

Simon advanced into the middle of the room. "I don't see why we have to rush."

"There's no hope for us," Mateo said before Simon could continue. "Don't delude yourself. Don't hope for a miracle. The end has come and gone."

"Mateo —"

"From the beginning we were a shipwreck. We were un-salvageable pieces that came together to form a whole. But we were never whole, not in a pure sense."

"That's not true. We fell in love —"

"I never really loved you."

Tears exploded in Simon's eyes. "That's a cruel thing to say."

"Staying was easier. It's always easier than making a break."

"You're being cruel, and only saying these things to push me away, to take away my hope."

"We lived in a dream-state. We weren't connected to each other, not in a *real* way. Christ, look at how many years of my life I've wasted. On you!" Mateo turned away from Simon. He knew he had been cruel. More than that, he had just proved that he had lost his humanity. But he was tired of being played for a fool, first by Liam, now by Simon. Somehow he had to get his power back, be in the truest sense manly by holding on to his will. The front door banged shut and Mateo looked in the direction of the hall. Simon was gone.

This is it. Mateo gulped his wine. He had struck the final blow, stood up for himself. This time the victory was his. Was it a victory? A hollow victory. No victory at all, actually, because he *had* loved Simon, worshipped him even. Simon's betrayal had sent his heart into ventricular fibrillation, and the only way to get his heart started again was to cut himself loose. That meant telling Simon that he meant nothing, to reduce him to nothingness. It came as no surprise that remorse and guilt quickly pinned Mateo down. How could he have been so cruel to the man he had loved more than life itself? He started to stand, as if he wanted to go after Simon, but couldn't. He fell back into the settee and polished off his wine. This was, perhaps, the worst moment of his life. He had lost everything that mattered to him. Now he had to find a way to reinvent himself and his life. Could he? He balked at the question, unsure of how to proceed.

4

"Who's the mother?" Zane spoke calmly as he held Melinda's hand.

"Promise me you'll remain calm when I tell you." Melinda tightened her grip on Zane's hand. "Zane…"

"Just tell me, Melinda," Zane said, gritting his teeth.

"Lisbeth."

"Lisbeth?" Zane yanked his hand from Melinda's and covered his face with it. "That —"

"Zane!" Melinda fell back into her chair. "You know how I feel about that word."

"Well, I didn't say it." He uncovered his face. "I can't believe it. I mean, I see her every goddamn day. You went to her baby shower." Lisbeth had studied law with Liam and Zane, and four years ago had joined his law firm in the tax department. He had met her son, Aiden, and it had never sunk in how much the boy, with his straight blond hair and wild blue-grey eyes, looked like Liam. Zane was trying to do the math. Could Aiden really be Liam's son? "Did he know she was pregnant before they broke up?"

"I don't think so. We all knew Liam was —"

"In love with your brother!"

"I'm going to let that slide because you're still in shock." Melinda took several gulps of her wine. "Zane…"

"I can't believe Liam never told me." Zane took his drink and made it vanish in two gulps. "Did he just abandon Lisbeth and Aiden?"

"My understanding is that they agreed that Liam wouldn't be involved. And I can't believe he would just abandon the boy."

Zane lifted his gaze to Melinda. "Does Mateo know? Don't tell me Mateo knew all this time and I didn't."

"No, don't be ridiculous." Melinda sat back in her chair. "But I plan to tell him."

"Oh, Melinda, don't do that. Isn't he going through enough already?"

"He deserves to know."

Zane bristled. "Is it your place to tell him?"

"When Liam's trying to get into his pants, yes."

"But what good can it do?" Zane stretched out his long hairy legs and crossed them. "You're overreacting. Mateo's not going to run to Liam. He's not that stupid. And telling Mateo about Aiden isn't going to keep him and Simon together. Mateo has to work all of this out for himself. Yes, it sucks, but that's life. Let him be for Christ's sake."

"Your language these days is —"

"Making you hot." Zane winked and reached for Melinda's hand. "I know you love Mateo but, please, don't do this."

The back door swung open. Mateo stepped onto the veranda, a full glass of wine in one hand and the open bottle in the other. He joined Zane and Melinda at the patio table, sitting down in the chair next to Melinda. "That was a train wreck," he said, and lifted his wineglass to his mouth.

Melinda sat up straight in her chair. "Where's Simon?"

"Gone," Mateo said.

"He loves you, Mateo," Melinda said with emphasis.

"What would you do if Zane cheated on you?" Mateo was trying to mimic Zane's contemptuous lawyer voice, purposely badgering his sister like a hostile witness at a trial, and Zane there ready to object. "Would you forgive him and let the marriage go on?"

"After I cut off his balls, maybe." Melinda curbed her urge to laugh as Zane uncrossed and crossed his legs.

"It's over between Simon and me. Over."

"And Liam?" Melinda raised an eyebrow.

Mateo rolled his eyes. "I told you —"

"There's a lot about Liam you don't know," Melinda cut in.

"Melinda!" Zane gave her a warning look.

"I don't want you to let him play you for a fool," Melinda said.

"I won't." Mateo looked at Zane. "You don't need to protect me. I appreciate it but I've known about Aiden almost since the beginning. After he was born, I mean."

Melinda's mouth dropped open, and she and Zane exchanged wide-eyed looks.

"You knew?" Zane said.

"You cannot look at that boy and not see that he's a replica of his father." Mateo gave a nervous laugh. "I mean, seriously, he could pass as Liam's double."

Zane, his face crinkled and knotted, was ready to explode. "How the fuck did you find out?"

"By accident." Mateo turned to his sister. "Do you remember that day you had to pick up Xavier from daycare because he was sick? You called me to go because you couldn't reach Zane and you were stuck in a meeting. Then you got out of the meeting but I had already left and you couldn't reach me. Xavier had a fever so we took him to the emergency room, and as we were heading into the hospital Lisbeth was leaving with her baby. He had an ear infection I think. I could tell that the baby was Liam's."

"But you didn't know for certain," Zane said.

"Only a fool wouldn't know," Mateo let fly and shrugged off Zane's piercing glare. "But he's never actually admitted it to me."

"There!" Melinda raised her closed fist in triumph. "That's what makes him a fraud. And that he hasn't had anything to do with the child."

"We don't know that," Zane almost shouted.

"Does it matter?" Mateo was dragging his index finger around the rim of his wineglass. "Isn't that between Lisbeth and Liam?"

"Maybe we should eat." Zane pushed his chair back and stood. "Are the steaks in the fridge?"

"Where else would they be?" Melinda shooed Zane away. "You have to stay away from him," she added once Zane had gone into the house. "Liam. He's no good."

Mateo took his sister's hand in his. "I will. I promise." He paused. "I told Simon I don't want the house. I think I might go away for a bit."

"Are you sure you want to throw that away?" Melinda's grip tightened. "Maybe you could reconcile. I'm not saying right away but with time."

"I know you're fond of Simon, and that you think he's a better match for me than Liam." Mateo set his wineglass on the table and placed his other hand on top of Melinda's. "But I'm telling you … Simon and me are done."

"Fine," Melinda conceded. "But do you have to run off?"

"It's an idea. Nothing's cast in stone, yet."

"We don't want to lose you," Melinda said with urgency. "And after what you said at Dad's funeral, about being a bridge —"

"That's another matter entirely."

"But you need to try. Tomorrow would be the perfect opportunity. We're all meeting at Mama's for dinner, before Benjamin and Betty head back to Toronto." She slipped her hand out of Mateo's. "Don't look at me like that."

"I think Benjamin and I will be okay," Mateo said. "I'll keep up contact with him. Mama and Ryan, well…" They laughed. "It's been an eventful few days, hasn't it?" Mateo let out a wry laugh, and the admission seemed to ease the tension building in his muscles. "It's funny how the trajectory of one's life can change so dramatically and so quickly." The tear creeping from his eye caught him off guard. "I told Simon that I never really loved him. I don't know why I said that."

"To hurt him," Melinda said disapprovingly. "You wanted to get back at him."

Mateo shrugged. "Maybe."

"I'm only going to say this one last time," Melinda said as she stood. "I don't think you should give up on Simon just yet. Sssh. I know what he did, and I can't imagine how much that could hurt but I feel…" She cupped her hand to his shoulder.

"Maybe it's not too late." She smiled. "Now, what's keeping that man?" she bellowed and strutted into the house.

Mateo emptied the remainder of the wine into his glass. *But it* is *too late.*

5

Simon, trembling, paced the area in front of the square silver-legged coffee table with a solid white melamine top. His eyes were moist but his face was finally dry. He had been moving back and forth across the dark brown rug for almost ten minutes without saying a word. All he could hear was, "I never really loved you," over and over again, like there was a scratch on the LP. The weight of the large hands on his shoulders made him stiffen. He spun around, raised his hands and pushed violently as the wet mouth came forward to kiss him. "Christ, I didn't come here for that," he said, taking a step back.

"Why did you come?" Kevin Milbrook said, unable to mask his annoyance, and sat down on the sofa.

With his hands in his pockets, Simon turned towards the window and stared into the black night. "Damned if I know." He breathed deeply. "I should go."

Kevin bounced off the sofa and moved to intercept Simon. "Maybe you need to let go … of him."

"How can I let go of him?" Simon's eyes were on fire. "I love him. Christ, I *love* him."

"But hasn't he moved on?" Kevin grabbed Simon's arm. "Hasn't he?"

Simon shook his head. "No."

"Don't be a fool."

"What am I supposed to do?" The question was instantly swallowed up by the empty air. "I can't simply cast him off and come to you." Simon shook off the ravaged looked on Kevin's oval face.

"You can't seriously still be in love with a man who told you that he never really loved you? Seriously?"

"He said that to hurt me." Simon yanked his arm out of Kevin's grasp. "He didn't mean it. He was angry."

"You're so fucking naïve."

"You don't get it because you've never *really* been in love."

"That's not true," Kevin spat. "I lo … I guess it doesn't matter now."

"No, it doesn't." Simon shoved his way past Kevin and made for the front door. Jiggling his keys in his pocket, he looked blankly at Kevin. "My coming here tonight was a mistake. I don't want to see you again." He rushed out into the warm night air, tears in his eyes again. He whipped out his cell phone and scrolled through his contacts until he came to JW, his contact from his cocaine days. Was the number still good? Simon's life was in chaos, he was in hell, at the bottom of that deep, black pit. He didn't seem to think that his life could get any worse and, hitting the dial button, didn't seem to care.

SUNDAY

1

THE DEEP BOOM OF THE DOORBELL LINGERED IN THE AIR, LIKE the last note of Alberto Ginastera's "Sadness" played fortissimo instead of pianissimo. Liam staggered, as if caught off guard, and held his breath. His mother was right. He wasn't moving forward. It wasn't even that he was stuck in neutral. He simply wasn't moving, stalled, like he had flooded the engine and couldn't get it started again. He had to *do* something, try to get himself and his life rolling again.

He glanced at the black Audi in the driveway, his heart racing, and rang the doorbell a second time. He was surprised by how key moments of his life flashed before him with each ding dong. The day he said to Mateo, "I love you, I've always loved you," and the horror shooting like daggers from Mateo's eyes. Running through the streets, billowing smoke chasing after him, as the World Trade Center's South Tower collapsed. Holding his father's hand as he passed from this world into the next. Handing his resignation letter to his boss who hated that he was gay and not interested in him. He heard the deadbolt turn over. Now he thought about his mother coming towards him, sporting her generous smile and arms outstretched. That was four short weeks ago as she welcomed him home at the airport. Home seemed so far away.

The door opened wide. Liam couldn't get his mouth to open and close. *Say something. Anything, goddammit!* It took a moment, but he managed to get out, "May I come in?"

There was a long silence.

"Sure," was the hesitant reply.

Liam, his eyes glued to Mateo's emotionless face, stepped cautiously into the house. He was nervous. Terrified, actually. He had rehearsed so many different conversations in his head, played out various scenarios as to how this meeting would unfold. The happy endings made him breathless. They gave him a will to live, reassurance of his purpose — to reclaim a lost love, himself and his history. Prove his worth. Change his life, his present. Heal this soul. Wasn't this the naïveté of an adolescent clinging to childhood dreams? He had lived through too many unhappy endings that almost suffocated him, crushed his spirit. It was time to take a stand.

Liam's heart sank as Mateo took up a position against the living room doorframe, a sign that Liam wasn't being invited in any further. What did that mean? *Has Melinda succeeded in turning Mateo completely against me?* He flinched at the coolness in Mateo's dark eyes. His chest tightened. Some days he wasn't sure if he had been a friend to anyone, and if he could be a *real* friend to Mateo again, whose doubting glare offered a brutal assessment: He's nothing but a fraud.

"I want to apologize," Liam said. "I know you think that it's too late for apologies, but I'd like to try anyway."

"It's not that it's too late," Mateo said dismissively, "but that it couldn't possibly matter now."

"It matters to me."

"That's because you're a narcissist."

Liam dropped his head and gritted his teeth. He felt two feet tall, like he was always under Mateo's thumb, never able to stand tall and to hold to his position. He looked up and sighed. "I realize now that coming back, without any warning and expecting you to let me into your life as if nothing had changed, was foolish. I never meant to hurt you, Matté, not now, not back then. Asking you to drop everything and go to New York was a stupid way for me to say, 'I love you.' Then cutting you off like that…"

"I don't need an apology."

"And I'm sorry if I came between you and Simon."

"Oh, for Christ's sake, Liam. The world doesn't revolve around you."

"I never said it did."

"You act like it does."

Liam gave a languid shrug. "All I want to do is find a way to make peace with you. I want you to look at me like I'm a person and not a bloody criminal."

"There you go again. Me, me, me. Can you even get through one sentence without saying 'I' or 'me' or 'I want?'" He shook his head. "And, Christ, Liam … my opinion, or my perception of you, shouldn't matter."

"But you know it does," Liam said, raising himself onto the tips of his toes. "Yours is the only opinion that *does* matter."

"Then you're not only a narcissist, you're also a fool." Mateo pushed off the doorframe and took a step towards the door. "I have a lot of work to do today."

"Matté, please…" Liam went and stood about a foot away from Mateo, and locked his gaze onto those brown eyes that both terrified and excited. In that moment those eyes terrified. Liam's heart thumped in his chest and his mouth became dry. He could smell the scent of mint on Mateo's breath and his memory flashed back to the day, a few months before he had left for New York, when he had been this close to Mateo. Closer even. It was New Year's Eve, and they were together at Parade Square for the outdoor concert. They were counting down to the New Year when Mateo turned to look at Liam. Liam could see Mateo's breath, caught its minty scent, and as the New Year dawned they were tussled about with the crowd, pushed momentarily against each other. Liam wanted to kiss Mateo then, hold him tight. There was a fuller, intense, aroma of mint as Mateo sighed, and a tingling sensation swarmed over Liam's body.

He wanted to kiss Mateo now. He touched his hand to the side of Mateo's smooth face, moving his thumb across the full lips that made him quiver. He thought Mateo would offer up some form of resistance, but there was none as he leaned forward and pressed his lips to Mateo's.

Liam stood there, his eyes wide open and his lips held to Mateo's, hypnotized and waiting for the dream to end. He slipped his arms around Mateo's waist and drew their bodies together, their belt buckles clinking against each other. He closed his eyes and jabbed his tongue into Mateo's mouth, and let out a soft groan. Just as the kiss was gathering momentum Mateo pulled away, but Liam managed to hold on to him.

Mateo dragged his hands out of his pockets and slid them between him and Liam. He pushed violently, and Liam released his hold. Mateo shoved his hands back in his pockets. "I don't really know what to say." He bit down on his lower lip. "A lot has changed in eight years. I've changed. You say you never meant to hurt me, back then or now, but you did hurt me, Liam. You're hurting me now. You walked out on me, on our friendship, and now you want what? For us to be friends? Lovers even?" He shook his head. "How fucked up is that?"

"Matté —"

"Mateo."

"Mateo, I —"

"No more excuses, Liam. If you could just, for once in your life, own up to what you've done."

"That's what I'm trying to do." Liam cupped his hands to the back of his head, breathed deeply, and dropped his hands to his sides. "I'm trying to be honest with you because I love you."

"I don't love you," Mateo said firmly.

Liam didn't believe him. "With everything that's going on —"

"Liam, I don't love you," Mateo repeated with conviction. "I could never love you because you've never been completely honest with me. And because of that I could never trust you, either."

"Mateo…" Liam blinked rapidly to stave off the tears ready to flood his eyes. "I want *you* to know everything about me."

"Everything?"

"Yes. Everything."

"Does that include Aiden?"

Liam could feel his legs about to give way, and as he started to collapse Mateo reached out to catch him but he was too heavy. They both fell to the floor. Mateo had put his left hand out to cushion the fall, just enough so that his bum hit the floor first before he fell backwards. His head narrowly missed the leg of the occasional table. Mateo tried to sit up but Liam was half on the floor, half on his stomach and waist. He rolled Liam off of him and sat up. He pushed himself backwards until his back hit the living room doorframe. Liam moaned, holding his left hand to his head as he sat up. His head was heavy although it had been cushioned by Mateo's stomach. The heaviness he felt was perhaps more embarrassment than anything else. He slid his body across the floor so that his back could rest against the wall of the staircase.

"Are you all right?" Mateo asked, the pain beginning to throb in his left hand.

Liam started to laugh, and as he was rubbing his hands over his cramping sides, tears flooded his eyes and rolled down his cheeks. "This is pathetic. I'm pathetic." He tried to dry his face with the back of his hands but the tears kept flowing. "My life has been one fuckup after another." He brought his knees up to his chest and pressed his head to the wall. "I wish…" His voice trailed off and he fixed his blurred gaze on Mateo. "How did you find out about Aiden?"

"I don't think that matters."

"Nothing seems to *matter* to you." Liam hid his face in his hands and stretched out his legs. There was that tightness again in his chest. He drew in long, deep breaths and pushed them out slowly through his nose. He uncovered his face and fixed his gaze to Mateo's chest, which made it seem like he was looking at Mateo when he wasn't. "Did I *ever* matter to you?"

"Yes, Liam, you mattered. You still matter to me, even though you shouldn't." Mateo lifted himself off the floor and, with his hand outstretched, took a step towards Liam. When Liam grasped his hand, Mateo pulled him up off the floor. Mateo had to jerk his hand free from Liam's. "It's too early for a drink, so how does coffee sound?"

"I should go. I mean, I've already made a complete fool of myself."

"So it can't get any worse."

Liam raised an eyebrow. "But, why?"

"Why, what?"

"Why would you want to spend any more time with me? Haven't I fucked up enough?"

"Liam —"

"Is it pity? Between you and my mother pity is the only thing on offer these days." Liam ran his hands through his hair. "I'm sorry."

"I'm not sure that means much coming from you at the moment," Mateo said, and made for the kitchen. He poured the remainder of the coffee between two mugs, added cream and sugar to one of the coffees and left the other black. Liam liked his coffee black. What an odd thing for Mateo to re-member about Liam after all these years. He picked up both mugs, carried them into the living room and sat down on the sofa. He placed the black coffee on the far corner of the cof-fee table so that Liam would have to sit in the armchair. Liam came into the room a short time later and, like an actor per-fectly taking direction, sat down in the armchair. "You know, Liam … you don't owe me, or anyone for that matter, an ex-planation. About Aiden, I mean."

"That's not true," Liam said, "not if I want to be honest with you." He picked up the mug and took a sip, and stared abstractly into the dark liquid as he searched for his words, the right words. Maybe what he said and how he said it didn't matter. Mateo didn't love him, and that truth, no matter how unsettling and maleficent, wasn't about to change. He set the mug on the coffee table and looked thoughtfully at Mateo. "I was one of those guys who didn't want to accept that he was gay. I did everything I could not to be gay. I went for counselling. I dated girls, and had sex with them. You can run, or try to run, from who you are but in the end the *real* you always wins out." He struggled to control the emotion in his voice. "I knew I was in trouble the first time I saw you. That was the first time I understood the true meaning of desire. But I was, at that point, still determined to kick the gay thing. I thought marrying Lisbeth would save me."

"Liam, it's not necessary —"

"But it is." Liam's tone was harsh, indignant. "I mean, I want *you* to understand that I didn't abandon Aiden. I didn't know Lisbeth was pregnant until after we had broken up, and she had already started dating Morgan when she found out she was pregnant. And Morgan…" Liam gave a wry laugh. Morgan Kelly had also gone to law school with Liam and Zane. "He was totally in love with Lisbeth before they had even started dating, and he didn't care that it wasn't his child. He wanted Lisbeth. That became, for me, the 'perfect' escape, but it wasn't what I wanted. I mean, I was prepared to offer whatever support I could for the baby, I mean, Aiden, but Lisbeth wanted me completely out of the picture. Could you blame her? What type of father would I have been anyway?

Whether it was the right thing to do or not, I gave up my parental rights, and took the job in New York." He shrugged. "Aiden has a good life. Yes, I told Melinda, and asked her not to say anything because my own mother didn't know, and still doesn't know. It would hurt her so much to know that I denied her her grandchild. It's called containment."

Mateo sat back in his chair. "I think you could have been a good father. Maybe that's a moot point since we can't change the past." He took a large gulp of his coffee. "You might like to think of it as containment, but now you're into damage control."

Panic settled over Liam's face already twisted out of shape by defeat. "What do you mean?"

"Zane knows about Aiden. So does Simon."

"Christ!" Liam's fingers curled into fists. "Melinda blabbed, didn't she? Fuck!" There was a silence. "At least now I know that Melinda really is against me."

"I think it's important that you talk to Zane, to let him hear your side."

"Melinda has probably brainwashed him —"

"Zane's his own man. Melinda doesn't think for him. Your return has proved that, created a sort of wedge."

"Fuck!" Liam bounced his right knee up and down. "My mother's right. I'm going to lose everyone."

"Talk to Zane."

"What about Simon?"

Mateo stood. "Who could Simon tell?"

Liam hesitated but said, "And you and Simon?"

"Why do you keep asking about Simon and me? It doesn't matter." Mateo ran his hand over his face. "Simon and me...

Relationships are complicated. Like any couple, we have issues. Nothing we couldn't handle until you appeared on the scene. Your presence simply brought the cracks to the surface. But that was more my fault that yours. Now that doesn't matter, either." Mateo took a step towards the door. "This week has put me behind schedule, and my publisher keeps hounding me —"

"Oh, right, sorry." Liam stood and followed Mateo to the front door where, one more time, they found themselves staring intently at each other. Liam wanted to be bold and kiss Mateo again, see if that could ignite something, but the awkward silence that inserted itself between them purged that urge. After Mateo opened the door, Liam said, "I am sorry, Mateo. I really am." He paused. "This is it, isn't it? I mean, you don't want to see me again, do you? Is it really impossible for us to be friends?" There was another silence and, after looking searchingly at each other for a time, Liam offered a faint smile and rushed out of the house.

MATEO STOOD AT THE DOOR AND WATCHED AS LIAM AMBLED down the walk and out of sight. Liam was right. Mateo, although he couldn't say it, didn't want to see him again. He couldn't risk it when the past was too alive in the present, too many misunderstandings smouldering underneath the surface. Friendship was impossible because Mateo didn't believe that Liam could stand *just* being friends. And Mateo didn't love Liam. He knew that now. The kiss should have aroused Mateo, made him feel something. But Mateo was completely limp, felt nothing, as if the spell had finally been broken. He could feel a new calm settling over him. While it felt like his world had crumbled down around him, maybe this was the moment where he could lay a new foundation, begin again. He closed the door and thought that maybe he had reason to hope for a brighter future. Then, as he passed by the living room entryway, he caught a glimpse of Simon's belongings that were stacked in the dining room.

Fuck!

Now he wasn't so sure.

2

"MAY I HELP YOU?" SUSAN SAID TO THE LONG-HAIRED brunette standing on the front porch.

"Mrs. Robertson, I'm not sure if you remember me. I'm Lisbeth Kelly. Well, I was Lisbeth Hall before my marriage." Lisbeth was holding the strap of her white purse in both hands, and nervously banged the bag against her shins.

"Lisbeth," Susan said, breathless, "do come in." Once inside, Susan offered Lisbeth a clumsy hug. "How are you, child?"

"I'm all right, thanks." Lisbeth tucked her hair behind her ears, which drew attention to her long, hooked nose. "And you?"

"I'm well, dear," Susan said to the woman who had nearly become her daughter-in-law.

"I heard Liam's back in town," Lisbeth said. "Is he here by chance?"

"Yes, he's back in town. No, he's not here." Susan shuffled Lisbeth into the living room, and they sat down on opposite ends of the sofa. "I don't know where he is. He was gone when I came downstairs this morning. Is there something I can help you with?"

"I'm not sure." Lisbeth's delicate fingers tapped her purse, which she held on her lap.

"Whatever is the matter?" Susan slid her body closer to Lisbeth, who let her tears roll down her freckled face. "Don't keep it all bottled up." Susan reached for Lisbeth's hand. "I'm not a complete stranger, you know."

"I know." Lisbeth smiled thinly. "You were always so nice to me."

Susan moved off the sofa briefly to retrieve the Kleenex box that was on the TV stand. She handed the box to Lisbeth, who pulled out a tissue and dabbed her eyes with it. Susan studied Lisbeth, whose round face was carved with lines that, up close, the foundation couldn't hide. *She's still so pretty.* Susan touched her hand to Lisbeth's thigh. "Tell me what's wrong, dear."

Lisbeth looked through her tears at Susan. "It's my son, Aiden. He's sick. Leukemia. He needs a bone marrow transplant."

"Oh, how awful. I'm so sorry, Lisbeth." Susan grabbed her hand. "Have you found a donor yet?"

Lisbeth shook her head. "Not yet. I'm afraid I'm not a match."

"Oh, dear." Susan blinked rapidly, trying to push down the tears pooling in her eyes. The thought of a sick child always made her emotional. Children were supposed to lead happy lives, not get sick. "What about the boy's father?"

"Well, you see..."

THE FRONT DOOR SWUNG OPEN. LIAM FROZE WHEN HE SAW Lisbeth on the sofa with his mother. *Christ, what now?* He hoped that the shock that had flared in his face had ebbed. He went into the living room and stood by the coffee table.

"Lisbeth," he said, rage flaring in his voice. "What are you doing here?"

"She came to see you," Susan said. "Her son is ill."

"Oh…" Liam ran his hands through his hair. "Mom, could you give Lisbeth and me a moment alone? Actually, never mind. Lisbeth, let's go for a walk." He returned to the front hall, opened the door, and waited for Lisbeth, who shared another clumsy hug with Susan before making for the door. Liam ushered her out of the house. He didn't say anything until they were several houses down the street. "Lisbeth, how could you!"

"Don't panic. I didn't tell her you're the father." Lisbeth grabbed him by the arm. They stopped walking. "Aiden's ill. Leukemia. And we need your help."

"Oh … that's … unfortunate. I hope he's going to be all right. But what can I do?"

"See if you'd be a good donor. He needs a bone marrow transplant." Lisbeth couldn't stop the tears from flowing. "Morgan, Terri and I have all been tested. We're not a match." Terri was Lisbeth's only child with Morgan. "You and Susan —"

"Susan?" Liam violently shook his head. "I'll get tested, but not my mother. I'm not dragging her into this."

"Liam, he's your son."

"That's why I'm willing to help. Just remember that, legally, Morgan's his father. I mean, does Aiden even know that I exist?"

"We just want to do everything to save him, to give him a chance at beating this illness." Lisbeth moved in front of

Liam and blocked his path. "What if you're not a match and Susan is?"

"One step at a time. Let me get tested. Then we'll talk…"

Lisbeth searched through her purse, pulled out a grey card and handed it to Liam. "Call that number to arrange your testing." She placed her hand to Liam's upper arm. "Thank you." She moved off down the street and disappeared.

Liam retraced his steps back to his mother's house. He wondered just how much Lisbeth had revealed to his mother. Was it enough that his mother might discern that he was Aiden's father? How would he explain that? He couldn't deal with that. He wasn't ready to deal with that. Inside, he moved quietly, hoping to go undetected. He was still heady with emotion from the kiss with Mateo and recovering from their conversation. *I could never love you*. That was definitive, and it cut through to Liam's core. He had, *une fois pour toutes*, lost Mateo, although Mateo had never belonged to him, and that devastated.

"That was quick," Susan said.

Liam jumped. He hadn't heard his mother come into the office. "Lisbeth always was dramatic."

"That wasn't drama. She's genuinely concerned about her son. And why would she come to see you about that?"

"We've remained friends." Liam avoided his mother's eye. "We didn't break up because I didn't love her…"

"It seems odd to me that she would —"

"She needed to talk to a friend. That's all." He could tell by his mother's narrow-eyed look that she was suspicious.

Susan picked up the photo of her and her late husband that was on one of the bookshelves and stared at it. Liam reminded her so much of him — their similarly hard dispositions and ability to keep their feelings boxed up. The only way to get the truth out of Wesley was to ask him pointed questions that made him squirm. She used to bombard Liam with questions during their nightly phone calls when he was still in New York. She'd let the silence linger, and he'd eventually answer. She returned the photo to its spot and fixed her gaze on Liam. "Do I need to ask where you were this morning?"

"Are you tracking my movements now? Are you one of CSIS's new recruits?" Liam sucked his teeth. "I had an appointment."

"You've never been a good liar." Susan backed up towards the door. "I suppose you were with Mateo." Silence. "Oh, Liam, when will you learn —"

"Well, he doesn't want anything to do with me. Satisfied?" There was a long silence during which Susan and Liam looked quizzically at each other. "I'm sorry. I've been saying that a lot lately."

"Liam…" She waited until Liam, who was rifling through the papers on the desk, looked at her. "Is it possible that I have a grandson that you've never told me about?"

The papers in Liam's hand slipped through his fingers and he lowered himself into his desk chair, a blankness blanketing his face. "Mom, I never meant —"

"Liam, don't," Susan said, her throat constricting and, with tears gushing from her eyes, turned and left the room.

Liam sighed. Just when he thought that things couldn't get any worse, they did.

3

"Thanks for coming." Mateo raised himself up slightly off his chair and extended his hand. The handshake was quick but firm, and a tingling sensation swarmed over his body. It wasn't the good type of tingling that made him feel buttery inside. He felt queasy, and thought for sure that he would throw up. Maybe that was a sign, although he wasn't sure what it meant. Lately, he wasn't sure what anything meant, if anything had a purpose. He reached for his wineglass and locked his gaze onto those metallic blue eyes. Something stirred inside of him. What was happening? Was everything that had been turned on its head about to be upended in a new way?

"I was surprised you called," Simon said. He peeled off his suit jacket and hung it on the back of his chair.

"To be honest, so was I," Mateo said.

They were at the Milltown Pub and Eatery, a popular destination for the Friday and Saturday night partygoers after the bars closed. But at two o'clock in the afternoon, Mateo and Simon had the place to themselves. Mateo's eyes moved with each sound that echoed through the space. Beyond the bar the open kitchen, and the faint sizzling sound of something touching the grill. The clatter of cutlery hitting the floor. The running of water.

Upon his arrival, Mateo had asked for a table at the back of the restaurant, away from the bar and entrance. He didn't want the staff eavesdropping on their conversation. But in the quietness, Mateo found himself listening to the wait and bar staff regale each other with stories from their dating lives, taking advantage of the lull in business. Mateo couldn't block them out, although he was trying to give Simon his full attention. But the staff's stories made Mateo want to laugh. They made love and commitment sound so effortless, nicely packaged up like a fairy tale. Mateo wanted to share his story, turn them against love and to a solitary life.

Simon flagged down one of the servers huddled at the bar. When the tall, dark-haired man with an eyebrow ring above his left eye approached the table, Simon ordered a rum and Coke and then levelled his eyes at Mateo. "Mateo…"

"Right…" Mateo took a large gulp of his wine and held Simon's gaze. "I'm not sure where to begin."

An outburst of laughter from the pub staff rolled over them. They felt as though they were disconnected from everything around them. Especially each other.

Mateo felt an unexpected giddiness as their gazes were trained on each other. He looked down, his eyes passing over Simon's round pink nipples that were visible through the white short-sleeve shirt that clung to his chest. This wasn't going the way he had planned it out in his head. He didn't know why it was so hard to talk to Simon. Maybe he did know why, but he thought that their history should have helped to build a bridge. He slowly lifted his eyes until they met Simon's. "I should have told you about Liam but it was easy to rationalize why I shouldn't tell you. By the time you and I had met, Liam was long gone from my life. I didn't want to relive that, open myself up to old feelings that I didn't understand. I'm sorry that I kept that from you. I just…" Mateo looked hopelessly at Simon. "You hurt me. You and Kevin —"

"I never meant for that to happen."

"But it did happen. At least once."

"Only once."

"Rum and Coke," the server said as he set the drink down in front of Simon. "Would you —"

"We're good for the moment," Simon said, somewhat abruptly, eager to be alone with Mateo.

Mateo massaged the left side of his forehead with his hand. "I don't know how I'm supposed to get past that, or how you think that you and I could be the same again. In less than a week our whole life has been upended."

"We have to take the long view."

"And what's that?"

"That love is patient and kind and protects and perseveres —"

"You're quoting scripture? Really?"

"I'm trying to say…" Simon paused to flush out the frustration that made his voice tremble. "I love you, Mateo. You need to believe that. I screwed up. I know that. It won't —"

"Don't say it won't happen again," Mateo cut in. "You can't guarantee that, not with your track record."

Simon sat back in his chair, trying to recover from the blow. He traced his index finger around the rim of his glass and drew in a deep breath. "Did you mean what you said? That you never loved me?"

"Simon…" Mateo looked down briefly. "I … I was angry and I wanted to hurt you like you had me. There was a time when I loved you —"

"But you don't love me now?"

"I don't know what I feel," Mateo said, pained. "So much has happened —"

"You mean Liam happened."

"Liam has nothing to do with us."

"Lately, he's had everything to do with us." Simon picked up his drink, drained it, and returned the glass to the table with a hard clank. "Have you and he, since his return, have you —"

"Oh, for Christ's sake, Simon." Mateo shook his head. "No, Liam and I haven't been together, not like that." He paused. "Liam did kiss me this morning."

"Oh, God," Simon moaned, leaned forward with his elbows on the table and hid his face in his hands. He breathed deeply, almost heaving. He thought he was going to be sick. He uncovered his face and looked blankly at Mateo. "And that's all that happened?"

"Yes. I don't love Liam. I don't want to be with him."

"So why am I here? It doesn't sound like you want to be with me, either."

"I don't know what I want," Mateo said in a loud voice that made the pub staff all swing their heads in his direction. He took a moment to calm himself down. "And I don't know what I feel. Logic tells me I should just pack up everything and run away. I ask myself how I can do that with everything that has happened in the past six days? It feels like someone pulled the pin of a grenade and tossed it into my life, and after the explosion I'm wading through the fallout, trying to pull out the shrapnel. I don't want to rush to make decisions that I may regret." He shrugged. "I had to see you today. After talking with Liam this morning ... I had to see if —"

"If you still felt something for me?"

"Yes."

"And?" After a long silence, Simon's eyes became moist. "I see."

The tall, dark-haired server appeared and collected Simon's empty glass. "Anything else?"

"Just the bill," Mateo said.

"Together or separate?" the server asked.

"Together," Simon said before Mateo could respond. The server disappeared and Simon added tersely, "I'll get it. It's fine." He set three five-dollar bills on the table.

Mateo reached over and grabbed his wrist. "I need some time, to sort things out, try to get grounded again." He removed his hand.

Simon's heart raced, a tingling sensation running roughshod over his body. Maybe this wasn't an end but a beginning? "I'll wait, no matter how long it takes," he said.

"You shouldn't have to wait," Mateo said in a conciliatory tone. "I mean, I don't want to tie you down, give you false hope only to leave you dangling."

"I'll wait," Simon repeated.

"I've decided to go away for a bit." Mateo polished off his wine. "I can't think here. There's too much noise in the background, too many distractions. Maybe while I'm gone you can stay at the house. It'd beat staying at the Express Inn. It is your house, too."

"How long will you be gone?"

"I'm going to play it by ear." Mateo pushed back his chair and stood. "I should get going."

Simon stood, grabbed his jacket off the back of his chair and followed Mateo out of the restaurant. Outside, the mid-day sun beamed into their eyes and made them squint. They walked in silence, heading towards Spring Garden Road, present and absent from each other at once. There were times during the course of their five years together when they sat quietly together in a room without speaking, their presence a bond and comforting. Words weren't needed. Was this one of those times? When they arrived at Queen Street, Simon said, "When are you leaving?"

"Monday."

"That's like, tomorrow," Simon said, panicked. He drew in a deep breath. "I don't have a key, remember? But I could stop by and get it now."

"Sure," Mateo said, suddenly unsure of his decision to let Simon stay at the house, but it was too late to change his mind.

Immured in silence, Simon and Mateo leisurely made their way to Bridges Street. Simon wanted to ask questions, find out where Mateo was going and what he had planned during his sojourn, but he was too afraid to break the peace. He couldn't shake the feeling that Mateo might never come back, and that terrified him. When he went through the front door, he staggered, horrified at how quickly Mateo had removed his imprint, cleansed the house of him as it were. He hadn't believed that Mateo had really packed up his things, not until he saw how the dining room was cluttered with his belongings. Something about it seemed to herald their finality.

Mateo, who had gone into the kitchen to grab the house key for Simon, came into the living room and handed over the key. He saw the disappointment in Simon's eyes but didn't know what to say. He went with, "I didn't touch your office."

Simon slipped the key into his pocket and made for the front door. Mateo came into the front hall and Simon said, "Should I wait until you leave before I —"

"Any time tomorrow. I leave early in the morning."

"Okay." Simon, tightly gripping the door handle, glared at Mateo, and they were both probing, searching, drilling for some semblance of truth. Simon smiled faintly, let go of the door handle and went over to Mateo. He reached for Mateo's hands and held them. He thought Mateo might try to pull away but there was no resistance. They just stood there, their eyes glued to each other in a trance. Then, in a bold move, Simon leaned forward and covered Mateo's mouth with his. He wrapped his arms around Mateo's body and backed him against the wall. They kissed, their tongues rolling over each other, panting, groaning, their eyes closed tight, tugging at each other's clothes.

4

ZANE GREY AMBLED UP THE WALK TO SUSAN ROBERTSON'S Flinn Street home. He had gone for a run to clear his mind, still grappling with the news that Liam was Aiden's father, and had not intended on seeing Liam. Liam was his best friend and had been his best man at his wedding. Even after Liam had moved to New York, they spoke regularly on the phone, like "two giddy teenagers," was how Melinda put it. They had become brothers, told each other everything, or so Zane thought. Now, with one secret that had been unearthed since Liam's reappearance, could anyone blame Zane for questioning the nature of their brotherhood? The foundation of their friendship was crumbling, and Zane wasn't sure that any type of repair could save it.

Zane stood on the front porch and stared blankly at the large wooden door. He was no longer certain if he should see Liam and try to speak to him. What would he say? And would Liam finally be completely honest with him? Zane hesitated a moment but eventually rang the doorbell.

The door opened wide and a red-eyed Susan, wiping the tears from her eyes, grunted, "Come in." The anger and hurt was twisted into her face. When Zane took two large steps towards her and drew her into him, she let herself cry. She pried herself out of Zane's hold after a few minutes and moved to close the door. Looking at Zane, her eyes narrowed and she folded her arms. "Did you know?"

"No," Zane said, and shoved his hands in his pockets. "I just found out."

"I don't understand how… It's just so cruel."

Liam came around the corner and sighed when he saw Zane. When he looked at his mother she immediately shifted her gaze away from him.

"Maybe you can get some straight answers out of him." She rushed into the living room, pulling the sliding doors closed.

"Do you want a beer?" Liam's voice was gruff. After his breakdown in front of Mateo earlier in the day, he was exhausted and wasn't in the mood for another confrontation. "Well?"

"Sure." Zane followed Liam down the hall.

In the kitchen, Liam grabbed two beers from the fridge, handed one to Zane, and led the way outside to the back deck. They sat down at the round patio table and avoided eye contact with each other. That went on for some time, until Zane couldn't take the silence any longer. "Melinda and Mateo have brought me up to speed."

"So you know everything and there's nothing else for me to say," Liam said, his voice bristling with sarcasm.

"Chuck the attitude," Zane said, and gulped his beer. "You could have told *me*, you know, about Aiden. Christ, you should have at least told your mother."

"Why is everyone making this about them?" Liam sucked his teeth. "It was between Lisbeth and me, and what we thought was, at the time, in the child's best interest. It was never about me or you or my mother. It was about Aiden, and giving him the best life possible."

Zane sat up straight in his chair. "You're his father."

"I'm not his father. I donated the sperm. Morgan is his father."

"Liam!" The shock thundered through Zane's voice. "Didn't you want to be his father?"

"No," was the forceful response that stunned them both, and they stiffened. Liam leaned back in his chair. "I've never had *that* desire. I've never had that paternal calling, not like you. I had enough trouble accepting who I was, am. Like I said, it was between Lisbeth and me and not the rest of the fucking world. No one was supposed to find out. Not for my sake but for Aiden's."

"I wish you would have confided in me."

"What difference would it have made?"

"Maybe I could have talked you out of abandoning him."

"I didn't abandon him. He'd have had to know of my existence for that. And you knew how Morgan was always after Lisbeth. He wanted Lisbeth. Period. At any cost. And from what I know he's been a good father to Aiden. That's all that matters."

Zane took another swig of his beer. "And now your mother knows."

Liam rubbed his forehead. "Lisbeth stopped by today looking for me. Aiden's sick. Leukemia, she said, and he needs a bone marrow transplant. She wants me to get tested to see if I'm a match."

"Will you? Get tested, I mean?"

"Yes. Of course." Liam rolled his eyes. "Do you think I'm that much of a monster?"

"Honestly, Liam…" Zane sat back in his chair. "When it comes to you right now, I don't know what to think. Melinda thinks you're a fraud, and I'm beginning to see her point of view."

"We're not all the infallible Zane Grey."

"You're certainly not the Liam Robertson I thought I knew." Zane set his beer bottle on the table. "I believe you love Mateo, that you've always loved him, but do you see what coming back here has done? Not just to you, but to Mateo and Simon, and your mother? I don't even know if you hear, really hear, the things you say sometimes." He stood. "Maybe you've convinced yourself that not being in Aiden's life was in his best interest, but deep down you know better than that. It was about you getting what you wanted. It's always about *you*. Coming back here wasn't about you making things right with Mateo, it was about *you* getting Mateo. Fuck, Liam … You're the only one in your world and to hell with the rest of us. How is anyone supposed to love you?" He waited for Liam to respond, as if daring him to, but Liam dropped his head. "You might have succeeded at coming between Mateo and Simon, but I won't let you come between Melinda and me more than you already have. You're not welcome at our home anymore, at least not until…" His voice broke off. At that point he felt like nothing he said would bring him and Liam closer to an understanding of each other. Zane backed away from the table and headed for the deck stairs. His long strides took him quickly to the side gate and away from the man he could no longer call a friend.

5

Mateo emerged from the en suite bathroom, naked, and went to recover his underwear. As he pulled on the white briefs he avoided eye contact with Simon, who lay on the bed with the covers pulled up to his waist. The sex had been rough and unusually vocal — Mateo uncharacteristically demanding submission and Simon eager to obey. Mateo wasn't sure why he succumbed to Simon's advances. Was it lust? Or was he hoping that sex could somehow change them, alter the trajectory of their lives? No, it was lust. Nothing more, nothing less. Pure horniness. And what disappointed the most was that, in the moment, it had felt so *right*. Now, in its aftermath, Mateo was searching for answers, and a way to wash off the feeling of filth and worthlessness clinging to his body like a scab unwilling to fall off.

Simon, pushing himself up in the bed, said, "Come here," and patted the empty place on the bed where Mateo had lain earlier. When Mateo went to pull on his jeans, Simon said, "Please, Mateo," trying to quash the harshness erupting in his voice.

Mateo let his jeans fall to the floor and climbed onto the bed, his back propped up against the headboard and his legs stretched out and crossed. He held his gaze to the dresser by the door and initially pulled his hand away at Simon's first play for it. At Simon's second attempt Mateo did not resist, and matched Simon's pressure. The silence, hanging large in the air between them, was like a stealthy lion waiting to attack its prey, and compelled Mateo to say, "I'm not sure this changes us."

"I know." Simon sighed. "But it was nice to be close again, to be with you." He let go of Mateo's hand and inched closer to him and, after hesitating a moment, wrapped his arm around Mateo's warm body. "Do you have a plan? I mean, for your trip?"

"No, not really." Mateo returned his gaze to the dresser. "I need to get away, far away. I need to get outside of this, to simply be in a different space." He cleared his throat. "I'm not sure I can stay here, in this house. I'm not sure I want to after everything that's happened. Not just what happened with you and Kevin, but with Liam being back and my father's death, I…" He blinked rapidly to hold back the tears gathering in his eyes. "This city may destroy me if I stay." He turned to Simon, delving deep into those penetrating eyes. *Maybe it is really over between us.*

Simon removed his arm from around Mateo and folded his arms across his hairy chest. "It sounds like you're not planning on coming back. Or if you do, that you won't be staying long."

"Maybe. I just … I don't know what happened to us." Mateo spoke with a deep sense of loss. "I don't know when we lost each other, when…" He censored himself, trying to hold on to his compassion. "Were you ever in love with Kevin?"

"No. *Never.*" Simon unfolded his arms and placed his left hand on Mateo's bare thigh, moving his hand gently back and forth. "I love *you.*"

"You can understand," Mateo said with an unexpected hostility, "why I might find that suspect, right?" There was a silence. "Do you think that we could seriously be happy again?"

"I'd like to think so, yes. A moment ago you said —"

"I was speaking metaphorically, or metaphysically..." Mateo sighed, then ran his tongue over his lips. "I'm not sure that I could ever trust you again."

Simon pulled his hand away and dropped his gaze. What could he say to prove that he was trustworthy? What could he do to prove his worth? "There's something you should know," he said, and looked up. "When you told me that you never really loved me, I ran to Kevin. I felt like he was my only ally. I talked, he listened. I just needed to vent. But we didn't have sex. When he tried to touch me I knew I had made a mistake by going to him and told him that I didn't want to see him again." He slid his body closer to Mateo's, their bare legs rubbing up against each other. "I'll do whatever it takes to prove that you can trust me again."

Mateo moved off the bed and stepped into his jeans. "I'm running late. Can you lock up when you leave? Thanks." He made his way downstairs, rushing to collect his keys and wallet and leave before he had to face Simon again. When he walked into the front hall, Simon was stepping into his shoes, and they looked intently at each other.

"So..." Simon raised his eyebrows and shrugged. "I guess..."

"I'm sorry," Mateo said.

"For what?"

"That things turned out this way."

Simon walked over to Mateo and stood close to him, so close that he could feel Mateo's hot breath on his face. "I'm not giving up on us. I told you, I'll wait. I meant that. I mean that." He leaned in to kiss Mateo, but Mateo took a step backwards. Simon made a sort of grunting sound and rolled his pursed lips, disappointment gleaming in his eyes. "I guess I should go." He made for the door, opened it slightly, and turned to face Mateo. "I'll see you when you get back."

"Sure."

"Be careful and safe."

"I will."

"If, at any time, you need —"

"I'll be fine, Simon."

"I love you." Simon waited a moment, staring dreamily at the only person he'd ever truly loved. Mateo, after a time, looked down, and that was Simon's cue to leave the house that was, perhaps still, *their* home.

Mateo lifted his gaze when the door banged shut. The silence had him backed into a corner, frightened him, sent him spinning. He was alone. *Alone.* Panic made his heart race. It felt like he couldn't breathe, couldn't catch his breath. He drew in long, deep breaths and his heart rate began to slow. He would go away. What other choice did he have? He had to come up with a plan for his life, figure out a way forward. He hoped that going away would bring some clarity to the situation, although he was beginning to have his doubts. Nothing made sense. How could his feelings for Simon ebb so quickly? Was he ready to give up the life he had made for himself? He was too scared, too naïve to believe that he was, *bon gré mal gré*, torn between Liam and Simon. Two loves, two very different loves that had succeeded at unmaking him. Maybe going away wasn't the answer. Staying away, putting down roots in some place new and foreign, where he could recreate himself, could be the only way for him to get back to himself.

Mateo checked the time. "Christ!" He moved across the hall and stabbed his feet in his shoes. He opened the door and turned back to survey the place he had called home. In that moment he knew that this wasn't home, and that it could never be home again.

6

Mateo sat in his car with the engine off, occasionally shifting his gaze in the direction of the red-brick house where he had spent his youth. It was almost six o'clock and although Melinda had not specified what time he was to be at Doris's house, Mateo knew there was a tradition of eating precisely at five. It was more than tradition. It was law. Did he have the courage to enter *that* house? Was he even welcome since he had failed, from Doris's perspective anyway, to "cast that demon out?"

The knock on the passenger side window made Mateo jump, and he turned the key in the ignition just enough to be able to unlock the doors. The passenger door opened and Zane climbed into the car. They shared a look of understanding and broke out laughing.

"Melinda sent me out to collect you," Zane said. "You've been sitting out here a while."

"I'm not sure I can go in there. I'm not sure I want to."

"Maybe it would do you good. Then you can at least say you tried. And if Doris does go all postal on you, flip her the bird and be done with it."

Mateo, with his head against the headrest, laughed. "How have you made it through all these years?"

"Strategy, my friend," Zane said grandly. "Strategy. And I take the longer view."

"So you're afraid Melinda will whip your ass if you were to say what you really feel…"

"And there's that, too." Zane, who had not closed the car door, slid his right leg out of the car. "Come on."

Mateo shook his head. "Oh, I don't think that I'm up for this."

"Remember, you have to have a strategy." Zane used his authoritative, and at times condescending, court room voice. "Eat slowly. Always have something in your mouth. It helps to censor yourself when Ryan or Doris are speaking. Make eye contact only with those you want to speak to."

"That's how you survived this family all these years?"

"Yes." Zane tapped Mateo's leg. "And three stiff drinks before arriving doesn't hurt, either. Now, come on before Melinda ends up out here and we both get an earful."

Mateo got out of the car and followed Zane to the house. He hesitated a moment before crossing the threshold. Inside, old memories rushed at him as the smell of lavender dominated. He had forgotten how much Doris loved lavender. Standing in the hall he critically surveyed the area around him to see what had changed. The reddish-orange carpet that had lined the staircase had been peeled away, replaced by a dark hardwood. The hall walls were still white and there was the faint scent of fresh paint. The framed picture of Jesus on the cross still hung on the wall but was faded. He turned slightly towards the living room where the piano remained pushed up against the far wall, used as a display unit for family photos. A quick scan of the photos revealed he wasn't in any of them.

The same grey sofa and loveseat, the ones his parents had bought the summer before he started university, framed the sitting area. In certain ways, it felt like time had stood still.

"We were about to give up on you," Melinda said as she charged into the hall. She hugged her brother. "How are you holding up?"

"Fine," Mateo said, and pulled away.

"All right, people," Melinda shouted and clapped her hands. "Everyone in the kitchen so we can say grace." The family assembled in the kitchen, still carrying on with their conversations until Melinda stomped her foot. As a hush fell over the room. "It's grace, not a prayer of confession," she said with emphasis, pointing at Ryan. "Keep it short."

There was a ripple of laughter.

Ryan lifted his hands in the air, and his tenor voice boomed, "Gracious Lord, we ask that You bless the food we are about to receive, that it will nourish our bodies and our souls. And we thank You, Lord, for Your comfort and strength during this difficult time. That You —"

"Amen," Melinda cut in.

"Amen."

Melinda looked at Ryan. "I told you to keep it short. Now, everyone, dig in."

As Melinda shouted out more instructions, Mateo stood off to the side as people grabbed plates and cutlery, and began scooping up food from the dishes and platters lining the countertops. He dodged the curious looks his relatives shot at him as they passed by, and that made him feel like he really didn't belong there.

Zane, who had been observing Mateo, came over and said, "What did I tell you about making eye contact with only those to whom you wish to speak?"

Mateo took the plate that Zane held out to him, and together they joined the tail end of the line queuing by the dining room entryway. Mateo's plate was less full than Zane's, who had taken a sample of everything on offer. They were the last of the adults to enter the dining room, and Zane took a seat between Melinda and Deidre while Mateo remained standing, eyeballing the empty seat next to Ryan with Doris to the right at the head of the table.

Melinda pointed at the chair. "Sit."

Mateo drew in a deep breath before sitting down. He took Zane's advice and immediately shovelled a forkful of food into his mouth. He looked at Zane, seated on the opposite side of the table, and winked. Mateo chewed thoughtfully, himself caught up in the mournful ambiance in the room.

"This mac and cheese is delicious," Deidre said at last.

Zane said, "Awesome," and drove another forkful into his mouth.

"Did you bring the mac and cheese, Aunt Deidre?" Melinda asked.

"Sure did," Deidre said, and let out a crowing laugh. "And it sure is delicious."

"Peter loved your mac and cheese," Doris said, choking on her emotion.

"That's all you're eating, Mateo?" Deidre said, shaking her head. "No wonder you're so skinny. You and Simon will have to come over to dinner so I can fatten both of you up." After gulping her ginger ale, she asked, "Where is Simon?"

At Mateo's wide-eyed look, she said, "Well, next week you bring him by for supper," as if commanding the troops. "I know he likes my mac and cheese, too."

"Aunt Deidre," Melinda said, "you sure are humble."

Laughter erupted around the table.

At the lull in the conversation Betty, who was seated on the same side of the table as Mateo, leaned forward and said, "Mateo, do you have another book coming out soon?"

"In the fall," Mateo said.

"What's it called?" Benjamin asked.

"My publisher and I are still trying to agree on a title." Mateo shot Melinda a hard look with a clear message: Don't go there.

"I can't wait to read it," Betty said, smiling.

"You don't even know what it's about," Ryan chimed in. "It could be some sinful, filthy —"

"Here we go," Benjamin said, shaking his head.

"Have you read any of Mateo's books?" Melinda asked sharply. "No? Then how would you know —"

"I don't read filth," Ryan said with disgust.

"Filth…" Mateo weighed that up. "Not to brag, but I've been nominated for several high-profile literary awards, and no one has ever used the word 'filth' to describe my writing. What, then, do you read? Picture books? Does that include *Playgirl*?"

Ryan, leaning backwards in his chair and to his right, looked warily at Mateo. "What did you say?"

"Mateo doesn't write filth," Deidre said. "Don't be such a bigot."

"Bigot?" Ryan's dark beady eyes widened. "Now just hold on there…"

"Peter would be so disappointed in you," Deidre said, her eyes locked on Ryan.

"Better than a night at Yuk Yuk's," Zane whispered to Melinda, who stomped on his foot underneath the table.

Mateo turned to Ryan. "You don't know anything about me or my writing."

"What on earth could you possibly have to say that's worth my time?" Ryan's tone was sharp and dismissive. "What I read reaches into the good in man, not darkness."

Mateo rolled his eyes. "Why is it that nothing changes with you? I don't understand how you can claim to lead those in following the ways of Christ when you continue to persecute me and others like me. If Christianity is supposed to be about love, where is yours? Where is the forgiveness? Most of all, where is *your* humanity?" He shook his head. "Christ, we sat at the back of the bus for how many years, and this is how we treat each other?"

The room fell silent, all eyes trained on Ryan and waiting for him to respond. He said nothing, his gaze held to his lap, his breathing heavy.

Doris broke the silence with, "God intended man to be with woman."

"I was taught that God created us all in His image," Mateo said. "That includes me, right?"

"Amen," Deidre said, and waved off Ryan's piercing glare. "God loves us all. It doesn't matter who we love. And that love is a blessing from God."

"Go on, Aunt Deidre," Melinda sang-spoke. "Preach it."

"I just pray," Doris said, looking at Mateo, "that you get yourself right with God."

"Wow." Mateo set his fork down on his plate and pushed his chair back from the table. "Nothing changes. Nothing ever fucking changes."

"Watch your language," Doris said sternly.

"It's a bit late for you to be telling me what to do or not to do, Doris."

"I'm your mother." Doris pointed her finger at Mateo. "Don't call me Doris. And this is my house."

Mateo threw his hands up in the air. "You win." He stood. He surveyed the faces staring at him, some with disdain, others with muted pride, others with relief. He felt a shift, a sort of reckoning, a strange feeling that calmed. "But I can forgive you. God made me gay, and that means He made you ignorant. I can't hate you for that. I can't hate you for your inability to love the way Jesus wanted us to love each other." He smirked. "It doesn't matter anymore that I'm not a part of this, that I'm not welcome here." He swiped playfully at Doris and said to her, with a combination of surprise and sarcasm, "I just got right with God," and walked out of the room.

Melinda caught up to Mateo as he was about to open his car door. She seized his hands and said, "Thanks for trying."

"You can't build a bridge without a foundation. And they're not interested in reconciliation, in getting to know *me*." Mateo sounded disappointed but secretly he was relieved. He felt no allegiance to his mother or Ryan, no bond. "They're holding stubbornly to their perceptions of me."

"I know," Melinda said, her voice throaty with emotion.

"But I have you and Zane and Xavier. You're my family."

"So are we," Benjamin said as he came up on his siblings. He was with Betty and Deidre. He extended his hand. "Don't forget that."

Mateo offered a firm handshake. "I won't."

Deidre moved to hug Mateo. "I'm so proud of you," she said into his ear. They pushed apart and she held his hands. "So proud."

Betty stepped forward and kissed Mateo on the cheek. "Come visit us." She reached for Benjamin's hand and, with Deidre following behind, went back inside.

Melinda flicked her eyebrows. "What about Simon?"

"Simon's moving back in, but don't get too excited. It's not what you think." Mateo jingled his car keys. "I'm going away for a bit. Simon's going to look after the house. Don't look at me like that. I can't stay here."

"You're running away," Melinda said.

"Maybe."

"Where are you going? What if we need to reach you? In an emergency?"

"Send me a message on Facebook."

Melinda placed her hands on her hips and cocked her head to the right. It was the pose she often took when they were kids on the school playground as she was about to put a beating on the guy who always bullied Mateo. "Really? You're going to give me attitude?" She stepped forward and drew Mateo into a clenching embrace. "Don't stay away too long," she whispered. "And don't give up on love." She pulled away and again trained her gaze on her younger brother. "Are you sure this is what you want to do? It seems drastic, and maybe —"

"I have to do this. I *have* to."

"All right," Melinda said, as if surrendering to the enemy. "Call me at least once to let me know how you're doing and that you're alive." At the silence, she added pointedly, "Or I swear I'll —"

"Oh, fine. I'll call you."

"Promise?"

"Promise."

"Cross your heart and hope to die?"

"Is that where Xavier got that from?"

They laughed and shared another quick embrace.

"I need to go pack." Mateo climbed into the car. He fastened his seatbelt and waited until Melinda had gone back into the house before flipping the engine. Then he sat there, staring blankly at the steering wheel.

He *had* to do this, that much he knew. Even if Melinda was right, that he was running away, this was his only course of action. He was running to himself, back to the man he thought he was and had dared to be. He would go home and pack, and slip away unnoticed. He had to go as much as he knew he had to come back. He'd have to find a way, somehow, to refashion home and his place in the world. That meant hanging on to hope, letting the light of hope reign over him. And he hoped that, upon his return, things would be different, that *he* would be different. There was always a risk that things would still be the same, and as much as that terrified him, he couldn't think about that now. He had to anchor himself to the present. Mateo shifted the car into drive and navigated his way through the quiet streets back to the Bridges Street house that had already become a very different place.

7

LIAM DIDN'T KNOW HOW LONG HE'D BEEN SITTING AT THE patio table. He shivered, felt the full veil of night pressing down on him, crushing him. He stared into the blackness that held, somewhere deep within, the promise of a brighter future, of a life worth living. Was that a possibility? Maybe. Only it seemed too far away, too far removed, and all Liam could see was the gaping void that threatened to tear him apart. After Zane had left, his mother tried to assure him that he would, with time, figure out a way forward, find himself. "Maybe this was your crisis-moment," she said. "And you survived. Now you have the chance to change your life, be bold. Don't be like everyone else. Don't pretend like you don't have a choice."

In the black sky, one or two stars flickered, like a candle at the end of its wick and about to go out. How much time was left before the light would go out forever, before everything possible became impossible? Did he believe that he could build for himself a life worth living? He knew he had to, quite simply, find a way to see whatever was directly in front of him, figure out the next right thing to do.

Aiden. Liam would, in the morning, call the number Lisbeth had given him and arrange to get tested. He would do what he could for Aiden while trying to remain anonymous. *Maybe Zane's right.* He reached for the wine bottle and topped up his glass. *This is* all *about me, about what* I *want. Maybe it always was.* "Does that make me a fraud?" he said into the warm, still air. His own answer surprised him. *Maybe.*

If only he had come back with a plan instead of trying to play it all by ear, as if he was adept at improvising, which he wasn't. He needed goals and milestones, ways to measure his success. Maybe that's what made him a fraud. While he still lacked a plan for his life, now he thought less about giving up law completely. *Goddamnit, Zane. Why do you have to be right all the time?* He was beginning to imagine setting up his own practice. That would keep him busy, occupy his mind. He had a few fences to mend, but was unsure if Melinda, more so than Zane, would be open to his apology. But he was willing to try. He felt a shift within him. Maybe he had survived his crisis-moment after all.

The patio door slid open, and Susan appeared on the deck, closing the door behind her before once again joining Liam at the table. "Are you going to sleep out here?" she asked.

"Maybe." Liam reached for his wineglass. "About Aiden…"

Susan waved her hands in the air. "I know you had his best interests at heart. There's just been so much loss, first with your sister, then to lose your father and …" Her rattled voice cracked and broke off. "I pray he'll be all right and I'll do what I can to help."

"You know he's a Robertson, and we're fighters. Aiden will be fine." Liam smiled faintly. "I'll talk to Lisbeth. Maybe there's a way you can meet him, that we can both meet him without upending his whole life, too."

"You know I'd love that," Susan said, a tear straying from her eye.

Liam chugged on his wine. "I think … once we know Aiden's … I don't think I can stay here. I don't think I should."

"Because of Mateo?" At the silence, Susan stretched her arm across the table and placed her hand on Liam's wrist. "I think you *have* to stay. Being here will be part of your process, helping you to get grounded. You have to accept that Mateo doesn't love you and you have to build your own life. You have to do that *here*, in spite of him."

"Everything just went so terribly wrong."

"Try seeing it as everything going as it had been planned for you," she encouraged.

"I don't believe in fate."

"You have to believe in something." Susan squeezed Liam's wrist and let go. "Don't stay up too late. You know how grumpy you get when you're tired."

They laughed, and Susan disappeared into the house.

But I can't stay here. Liam, for the first time since his return, was certain of at least that one thing. Being so close to Mateo yet unable to go to him, be with him, touch him … Staying would destroy Liam, break him down bit by bit. He had to build himself up again, be his own hero. To do that meant putting down roots elsewhere. It didn't have to be a far-away place. He knew that now. But a place where he wouldn't risk running into Mateo, where he wouldn't have to relive that pain. Maybe he could get a cosy cottage in Peggy's Cove or Mahone Bay, and live a quiet, solitary life. Like a monk. Only with sex. He'd be close enough to be around if his mother, or Aiden, needed him. Was he ready to be a father, or some type of parental figure? The question terrified him, made his heart thump in his chest.

Liam polished off his wine, stood, and carried the empty glass into the house. A short time later he lay in his bed, his hands cupped to the back of his head and staring into the blackness that held, somewhere deep within, the promise of a brighter future, of a life worth living. Was that a possibility? Maybe. Only it seemed too far away, too far removed, but clearly visible was the gaping void beginning to tear him apart. He closed his eyes and hoped that, when he woke up in the morning, he'd have the courage to be bold, to change his life in a meaningful way.

MONDAY

MATEO JAMMED THE KEY IN THE DOOR AND STOOD THERE, immobile, unsure as to his next move. Should he enter the house? Should he back away before his presence was detected? He closed his eyes and took several long, deep breaths, slowly pushing each one out through his nose. What awaited him on the other side of the door and did he want to find out? He waited, counted backwards from ten, then opened his eyes. He walked into the house.

Inside, the stony silence welcomed him, and as he set his suitcase down on the floor by the hall closet he could feel the anxiousness, so long knotted in his muscles, begin to abate. No sign of Simon. Mateo closed the door and kicked off his shoes, and then went into the living room. It wasn't the same house that he had left five weeks ago. Order had been restored to the dining room, Simon's possessions had returned to the spaces they had occupied previously — proof of his presence in the house restored. Mateo went through the dining room and into the kitchen. The counters were clean, the sink empty, the stove spotless, as if it were a model kitchen for display purposes only. Simon wasn't much of a cook. Had he eaten out the entire time Mateo was gone? Mateo opened the fridge. It was bare.

He moved out of the kitchen and down the hall to his office, surprised to find that the door was open. He had closed it before he left, thought that it would be a clear sign to leave his space undisturbed. He entered the room lit up by the afternoon sun streaming in through the windows. He went over to his desk and rummaged through the envelopes neatly piled on it, separated according to size. He was about to sit down when the bang of a car door closing startled him. He turned towards the window facing east and swallowed hard. He saw Simon, standing next to his car, place his hand on the hood. He spun around, levelled his eyes at Mateo's office window, then ran up the walk. Mateo didn't flinch. He knew this was his now-or-never moment. He made his way towards the front hall, arriving just as the front door opened.

Inside, Simon froze when he saw the grey suitcase on the floor and then looked up, a broad smile spreading across his face. "Mateo!" He leaned his brown leather satchel against Mateo's suitcase and rushed to Mateo, whom he hugged tightly. He lifted Mateo up off the floor, spun him around and set him back down again. He took a step back. "You're home. *Finally*."

Beep, beep, beep, beep. Mateo rolled over and reached out into the darkness, his hand flopping about the nightstand until it connected with the clock and the beeping stopped. He propped himself up in the bed, his head heavy, almost spinning, as if he were drunk. But it was the shock of being awakened from a deep sleep. And a dream that felt real, like he had lived through it all. Was it just a dream or was it real? He reached out and patted the other side of the bed, which was empty. It *was* a dream.

His eyes were slow to focus, and when he saw the time on the clock he groaned. Four thirty. He had to leave in an hour in order to make his eight o'clock flight, yet he lay there, staring into the darkness, his mind in an anxious tumult. Yesterday, after the scene with his mother, he felt certain that he had to leave. He came home, booked a flight and packed his suitcase. Now there had been a shift, and he was trying to decipher it, pin it down. A transformation of sorts. An awakening. The world as he knew it had changed, and him along with it. Was that a good thing?

Mateo pushed back the counterpane and got out of the bed. He showered and dressed, and placed the last few items — his travel kit, cell phone charger, extra batteries for his camera — into his suitcase and closed it. He moved slowly, like there wasn't a need to rush. He picked up his suitcase and went downstairs, dropping his bag on the floor by the hall closet. He headed for the kitchen and turned on the light. He had pre-programmed the coffeemaker before going to bed. He poured himself a mug and sat down at the breakfast nook table.

He took a sip of his coffee. It lodged in his throat, and he couldn't decide whether to swallow it or spit it back into his mug. He swallowed and winced, the liquid burning his throat and making him cough. The bitter taste was foreign to him. Mateo looked at the dark liquid in the mug. He hadn't added cream or sugar to his coffee, which was his ritual. He wasn't himself. He didn't know who he was. Not now, not with his life hanging in the balance. He set his coffee mug aside, placed his arms on the table and leaned forward, resting his head on his forearms. He closed his eyes and, for the first time since the news of his father's death, felt a sense of peace.

Mateo opened his eyes again, crusty and heavy. He sat up straight and stiffened. The morning sun beamed in through the windows. A white film had formed on the surface of his coffee. He fixed his gaze on the microwave clock and shook his head. Seven minutes past nine. He had missed his flight, and that didn't seem to bother him, not in the way that he thought it should.

He got up from the table and, carrying his coffee mug, went over to the sink and poured out the liquid. He rubbed his eyes, trying to sweep away the sleep. He was on his way to the bathroom when the front door swung open. Mateo staggered backwards, as if he were going to back out of the hall without being seen.

Simon, struggling to get his two large suitcases through the door, froze when he saw the grey suitcase on the floor and looked up. Was he dreaming? He said, "Mateo?" His heavy bags crashed to the floor with a loud thud. "You said … I thought…"

"I missed my flight." Mateo advanced into the hall and moved his suitcase so that Simon could come more fully into the house.

"I'll be right back," Simon said and slipped out of the house. He reappeared moments later carrying his satchel. He tossed the bag on the floor next to his suitcases and closed the front door. He kicked off his shoes and started to panic when he realized Mateo had vanished. "Mateo," he called out to the moody walls, but there was no response. "Mateo!" In the silence came the flushing of the toilet at the end of the hall, followed by the running of water in the sink. Simon paced the hall until Mateo returned. They couldn't help but look searchingly at each other, wondering if now there was understanding where there had been none. "Is there any coffee?" he said and cringed because he didn't know what else to say.

Mateo said, "I'll make a fresh pot."

Simon followed Mateo into the kitchen. He watched Mateo, with his back always to him, move about the kitchen, and pretending as if he were alone. Simon didn't feel, however, like he was cut off. This was very real. He knew that this was his moment, when he had to get Mateo to talk to him, about their future, or he risked losing everything. Simon waited for Mateo to move away from the coffeemaker before collecting the mug that Mateo had poured out for him. Mateo sat down at the breakfast nook table and Simon joined him. "I'm sorry you missed your flight. But I'm really happy to see you, that you're here."

"I wanted to leave. I planned to leave. Melinda said I'd be running away." Mateo sat with his gaze focused on his mug. "She was right. I thought I could go anyway, but when I got up this morning and…" He looked at Simon. "I've been running so long. I'm exhausted."

Simon reached out and placed his hand on top of Mateo's. "Then stop running."

"I tried," Mateo said, his eyes becoming moist, "to be a bridge, to give life to what I said at Peter's funeral but…" He gently pulled his hand from underneath Simon's and sat back in his chair. "How can you build a bridge when there's no foundation, no support?"

Simon scrunched his eyebrows. "Did you actually go —"

"To see my 'family?' Yes." Mateo gave a wry laugh. "As fucking stupid as it was, I accepted Melinda's invitation to dine with the righteous, holier-than-thou, Borden clan. Christ, they're like a cult. Worse than Branch Davidians." He took a sip of his coffee. "Whoever said blood is thicker than water should be shot. No, they should be water boarded. Christ, they should *suffer*."

Simon burst out laughing. "I'm sorry. It's not funny. Well, just a little. I never noticed the dimples in your cheeks before when you're angry. It's too cute." He tried to stifle his laugh but had difficulty bringing it under control. "I'm sorry. Please, don't look at me like that. It's just … you're *here*, and we're talking in a real way, and I'm happy about that."

Mateo brought himself forward and sat with his forearms resting on the table and his hands loosely wrapped around his mug. "I don't know what's next for us." Mateo heard how "us" lingered in the air, and was surprised by how he so easily anchored himself to it.

"I know," Simon said. "But I think that you and I have a foundation. There are a couple of cracks —"

"A couple?" Mateo's eyes widened.

"Fine. There are a lot of cracks that have to be filled, but I'm willing to try, to do whatever it is that *you* want me to do. You know, Mateo, I'm —"

"I don't want to hear 'I'm sorry' again," Mateo said. "You've said that, repeatedly, and I know you meant it but it doesn't move us forward." There was that "us" again, and did that somehow make them real? Mateo was caught off guard by his silent answer: Yes. He reached for Simon's hand, applied a little pressure, and added, "Melinda also encouraged me to not give up on love. As much as I've wanted to hate you, make you feel the same type of pain that you caused me,

I couldn't do that. I wanted to but I couldn't. And you can thank Liam for that. Let me finish. I was really hard on Liam. Once all the cards were on the table, once he and I said good-bye, I first felt sorry for him and then I felt guilty. I thought that I should have tried harder to see his point of view. I showed no compassion, and if I do the same with you …" He smiled faintly. "I may have lost my humanity, but I certainly don't want to live in a world without forgiveness. And I'm not saying that I forgive you yet. Christ, that'll take some time. But I'm willing to try."

Simon matched the pressure of Mateo's grip. "I think that proves that you haven't lost your humanity." He opened his mouth to speak but his words clogged up at the back of his throat. He eventually managed to get out, "Do you think … should we … what about couple therapy?"

"Maybe." Mateo let go of Simon's hand. "It could prove useful, finally free you of all your idiosyncrasies."

"Hey!" They laughed. "More coffee?"

"Sure," Mateo said. There was something about Simon's frantic movements that made Mateo smile, and created an un-expected flurry of emotion. His stomach flipped. He did after all still *feel* something for Simon, but it was too hard, or too soon, to say if what he felt was love. Was it desire? Simon came back to the table and he was, in his blue short-sleeved shirt that hugged his torso and the dark-blue dress pants that were snug against his round ass, deceptively charming, de-ceptively sexy. When had Simon dyed the grey out of his full mane? He looked younger, more confident. Was he trying to impress someone? Simon was smiling every time he looked at Mateo, and that made the hair on Mateo's arms stand up. Was

Mateo falling in love all over again? "This afternoon I'll clear out the dining room, put your things back where they were."

"I'll help."

"Simon…" Mateo spoke slowly, emphasizing each word. "If, as you said, that love is patient and kind, then all I ask is that you be patient with me. I do want to work through this. I don't want to give up on us without trying. But … I'd be lying if I said I wasn't a little uncertain about what it is that I actually want. But like I said, I'm willing to try, to see if we can renew our love. It might just take time."

"I know," Simon said. "And I appreciate that. Whatever you need, be it space, time, anything, please just tell me."

Mateo nodded. "Aunt Deidre was asking where you were yesterday. For some ungodly reason she's always liked you."

"Hey…"

They laughed. It felt good to laugh, to share a certain alliance.

"She wants us to come over for dinner," Mateo said.

Simon licked his lips. "I love her mac and cheese."

"I'll call her later and set something up."

"I'd like that."

Mateo contemplated the man who had once made his heart race, and now, in that moment, his heartbeat was gaining momentum. Mateo took Simon's hand in his and squeezed it. Silence moved in and had dominion over them. Words weren't needed. Here, again, simply their presence was a bond.

Why is it that I want to pull away? Mateo winked. *Is that why he's hanging on so tightly to my hand? Can he sense me wanting to pull away?* He realized then that the handholding was necessary, like it was the only thing holding them together in the moment and their love depended on it. This was different. Mateo felt different. This house that he thought could never be home again *was* home, and it was so good to be back in the home he had built with the man he *did* love — to be, in a new and different way, *together*. But this was the first step. Joy was in knowing that they had not abandoned each other, or left their love to asphyxiate itself. And Mateo knew that Simon would do whatever was necessary to make it work. So would Mateo. He wasn't ready to give up on love.

Mateo didn't move when Simon leaned in to kiss him. He found himself immediately swept up in the kiss, like he couldn't get enough, like everything old was in fact new again. He smiled as they kissed and they both broke out laughing. They leaned back in their chairs and stared intently at each other. Mateo knew that Simon was right. Love *is* patient and kind, and with time, much patience and *love*, they would be all right.

And Mateo couldn't wait to see what came next.

ACKNOWLEDGEMENTS

I want to thank Dave Taylor of thEditors for his valuable insights that helped me to make this the best story possible. I am also deeply indebted to my good friend Adrienne Ascah, who graciously agreed to read this manuscript. Adrienne's sharp eye and critical feedback proved, one more time, invaluable.

Many thanks as always to Suzanne Robinson, Heather-Anne Gillis and Myrtle Gillis for their constant friendship and for always believing in me.

Special thanks to John Fortier for being who you are.

ABOUT THE AUTHOR

MARCUS LOPÉS is the author of *Everything He Thought He Knew*, first published as *Freestyle Love* in 2011 by LazyDay Publishing. In 2017, he made the leap into self-publishing with *The Flowers Need Watering*. An avid runner and amateur chef/baker, he lives in Toronto, Ontario. For more information, you can visit his website at marcuslopes.ca. You can also follow him on Facebook and Twitter.

Made in the USA
Monee, IL
31 May 2020

32267415R00178